Always Outnumbered, Always Outgunned

Walter Mosley

W F HOWES LTD

This large print edition published in 2002 by
W F Howes Ltd
Units 6/7, Victoria Mills, Fowke Street
Rothley, Leicester LE7 7PJ

1 3 5 7 9 10 8 6 4 2

First published in the United Kingdom
in 1997 by Serpent's Tail

A CIP catalogue record for this book is available
from the British Library

ISBN 1 84197 566 4

Typeset by Palimpsest Book Production Limited,
Polmont, Stirlingshire
Printed and bound in Great Britain
by Antony Rowe Ltd, Chippenham, Wilts.

FOR GLORIA LOOMIS

CONTENTS

WITH SPECIAL THANKS
TO JULIE GRAU

Always Outnumbered,
Always Outgunned

CRIMSON SHADOW

1

'What you doin' there, boy?'

It was six a.m. Socrates Fortlow had come out to the alley to see what was wrong with Billy. He hadn't heard him crow that morning and was worried about his old friend.

The sun was just coming up. The alley was almost pretty with the trash and broken asphalt covered in half-light. Discarded wine bottles shone like murky emeralds in the sludge. In the dawn shadows Socrates didn't even notice the boy until he moved. He was standing in front of a small cardboard box, across the alley – next to Billy's wire fence.

'What bidness is it to you, old man?' the boy answered. He couldn't have been more than twelve but he had that hard convict stare.

Socrates knew convicts, knew them inside and out.

'I asked you a question, boy. Ain't yo' momma told you t'be civil?'

'Shit!' The boy turned away, ready to leave. He

wore baggy jeans with a blooming blue T-shirt over his bony arms and chest. His hair was cut close to the scalp.

The boy bent down to pick up the box.

'What they call you?' Socrates asked the skinny butt stuck up in the air.

'What's it to you?'

Socrates pushed open the wooden fence and leapt. If the boy hadn't had his back turned he would have been able to dodge the stiff lunge. As it was he heard something and moved quickly to the side.

Quickly. But not quickly enough.

Socrates grabbed the skinny arms with his big hands – the rock breakers, as Joe Benz used to call them.

'Ow! Shit!'

Socrates shook the boy until the serrated steak knife, which had appeared from nowhere, fell from his hand.

The old brown rooster was dead in the box. His head slashed so badly that half of the beak was gone.

'Let me loose, man.' The boy kicked, but Socrates held him at arm's length.

'Don't make me hurt you, boy,' he warned. He let go of one arm and said, 'Pick up that box. Pick it up!' When the boy obeyed, Socrates pulled him by the arm – dragged him through the gate, past the tomato plants and string bean vines, into the two rooms where he'd stayed since they'd let him out of prison.

★　　★　　★

The kitchen was only big enough for a man and a half. The floor was pitted linoleum; maroon where it had kept its color, gray where it had worn through. There was a card table for dining and a fold-up plastic chair for a seat. There was a sink with a hot plate on the drainboard and shelves that were once cabinets – before the doors were torn off.

The light fixture above the sink had a sixty-watt bulb burning in it. The room smelled of coffee. A newspaper was spread across the table.

Socrates shoved the boy into the chair, not gently.

'Sit' own!'

There was a mass of webbing next to the weak lightbulb. A red spider picked its way slowly through the strands.

'What's your name, boy?' Socrates asked again.

'Darryl.'

There was a photograph of a painting tacked underneath the light. It was the image of a black woman in the doorway of a house. She wore a red dress and a red hat to protect her eyes from the sun. She had her arms crossed under her breasts and looked angry. Darryl stared at the painting while the spider danced above.

'Why you kill my friend, asshole?'

'What?' Darryl asked. There was fear in his voice.

'You heard me.'

'I-I-I didn't kill nobody.' Darryl gulped and

opened his eyes wider than seemed possible. 'Who told you that?'

When Socrates didn't say anything, Darryl jumped up to run, but the man socked him in the chest, knocking the wind out of him, pushing him back down in the chair.

Socrates squatted down and scooped the rooster up out of the box. He held the limp old bird up in front of Darryl's face.

'Why you kill Billy, boy?'

'That's a bird.' Darryl pointed. There was relief mixed with panic in his eyes.

'That's my friend.'

'You crazy, old man. That's a bird. Bird cain't be nobody's friend.' Darryl's words were still wild. Socrates knew the guilty look on his face.

He wondered at the boy and at the rooster that had gotten him out of his bed every day for the past eight years. A rage went through him and he crushed the rooster's neck in his fist.

'You crazy,' Darryl said.

A large truck made its way down the alley just then. The heavy vibrations went through the small kitchen, making plates and tinware rattle loudly.

Socrates shoved the corpse into the boy's lap. 'Get ovah there to the sink an' pluck it.'

'Shit!'

'You don't have to do it . . .'

'You better believe I ain't gonna . . .'

'. . . but I *will* kick holy shit outta you if you don't.'

4

'Pluck what? What you mean, pluck it?'

'I mean go ovah t'that sink an' pull out the feathers. What you kill it for if you ain't gonna pluck it?'

'I'as gonna sell it.'

'Sell it?'

'Yeah,' Darryl said. 'Sell it to some old lady wanna make some chicken.'

2

Darryl plucked the chicken bare. He wanted to stop halfway but Socrates kept pointing out where he had missed and pushed him back toward the sink. Darryl used a razor-sharp knife that Socrates gave him to cut off the feet and battered head. He slit open the old rooster's belly and set aside the liver, heart, and gizzard.

'Rinse out all the blood. All of it,' Socrates told his captive. 'Man could get sick on blood.'

While Darryl worked, under the older man's supervision, Socrates made Minute rice and then green beans seasoned with lard and black pepper. He prepared them in succession, one after the other on the single hot plate. Then he sautéed the giblets, with green onions from the garden, in bacon fat that he kept in a can over the sink. He mixed the giblets in with the rice.

When the chicken was ready he took tomatoes, basil, and garlic from the garden and put them all in a big pot on the hot plate.

'Billy was a tough old bird,' Socrates said. 'He gonna have to cook for a while.'

'When you gonna let me go, man?'

'Where you got to go?'

'Home.'

'Okay. Okay, fine. Billy could cook for a hour more. Let's go over your house. Where's that at?'

'What you mean, man? You ain't goin' t'my house.'

'I sure am too.' Socrates said, but he wasn't angry anymore. 'You come over here an' murder my friend an' I got to tell somebody responsible.'

Darryl didn't have any answer to that. He'd spent over an hour working in the kitchen, afraid even to speak to his captor. He was afraid mostly of those big hands. He had never felt anything as strong as those hands. Even with the chicken knife he was afraid.

'I'm hungry. When we gonna eat?' Darryl asked. 'I mean I hope you plan t'eat this here after all this cookin'.'

'Naw, man,' Socrates said. 'I thought we could go out an' sell it t'some ole lady like t'eat chicken.'

'Huh?' Darryl said.

The kitchen was filling up with the aroma of chicken and sauce. Darryl's stomach growled loudly.

'You hungry?' Socrates asked him.

'Yeah.'

'That's good. That's good.'

6

'Shit. Ain't good 'less I get sumpin' t'eat.'

'Boy should be hungry. Yeah. Boys is always hungry. That's how they get to be men.'

'What the fuck you mean, man? You just crazy. That's all.'

'If you know you hungry then you know you need sumpin'. Sumpin' missin' an' hungry tell you what it is.'

'That's some kinda friend to you too?' Darryl sneered. 'Hungry yo' friend?'

Socrates smiled then. His broad black face shone with delight. He wasn't a very old man, somewhere in his fifties. His teeth were all his own and healthy, though darkly stained. The top of his head was completely bald; tufts of wiry white hovered behind his ears.

'Hungry, horny, hello, and how come. They all my friends, my best friends.'

Darryl sniffed the air and his stomach growled again.

'Uh-huh,' Socrates hummed. 'That's right. They all my friends. All of 'em. You got to have good friends you wanna make it through the penitentiary.'

'You up in jail?' Darryl asked.

'Yup.'

'My old man's up in jail,' Darryl said. 'Least he was. He died though.'

'Oh. Sorry t'hear it, li'l brother. I'm sorry.'

'What you in jail for?'

Socrates didn't seem to hear the question. He

7

was looking at the picture of the painting above the sink. The right side of the scene was an open field of yellow grasses under a light blue sky. The windows of the house were shuttered and dark but the sun shone hard on the woman in red.

'You still hungry?' Socrates asked.

Darryl's stomach growled again and Socrates laughed.

3

Socrates made Darryl sit in the chair while he turned over the trash can for his seat. He read the paper for half an hour or more while the rooster simmered on the hot plate. Darryl knew to keep quiet. When it was done, Socrates served the meal on three plates – one for each dish. The man and boy shoveled down dirty rice, green beans, and tough rooster like they were starving men; eating off the same plates, neither one uttered a word. The only drink they had was water – their glasses were mayonnaise jars. Their breathing was loud and slobbery. Hands moved in syncopation; tearing and scooping.

Anyone witnessing the orgy would have said that they hailed from the same land; prayed to the same gods.

When the plates were clean they sat back bringing hands across bellies. They both sighed and shook their heads.

'That was some good shit,' Darryl said. 'Mm!'

'Bet you didn't know you could cook, huh?' Socrates asked.

'Shit no!' the boy said.

'Keep your mouth clean, li'l brother. You keep it clean an' then they know you mean business when you say sumpin' strong.'

Darryl was about to say something but decided against it. He looked over at the door, and then back at Socrates.

'Could I go now?' he asked, a boy talking to his elder at last.

'Not yet.'

'How come?' There was an edge of fear in the boy's voice. Socrates remembered many times reveling in the fear he brought to young men in their cells. Back then he enjoyed the company of fear.

'Not till I hear it. You cain't go till then.'

'Hear what?'

'You know what. So don't be playin' stupid. Don't be playin' stupid an' you just et my friend.'

Darryl made to push himself up but abandoned that idea when he saw those hands rise from the table.

'You should be afraid, Darryl,' Socrates said, reading the boy's eyes. 'I kilt men with these hands. Choked an' broke 'em. I could crush yo' head wit' one hand.' Socrates held out his left palm.

'I ain't afraid'a you,' Darryl said.

'Yes you are. I know you are 'cause you ain't no

fool. You seen some bad things out there but I'm the worst. I'm the worst you ever seen.'

Darryl looked at the door again.

'Ain't nobody gonna come save you, li'l brother. Ain't nobody gonna come. If you wanna make it outta here then you better give me what I want.'

Socrates knew just when the tears would come. He had seen it a hundred times. In prison it made him want to laugh; but now he was sad. He wanted to reach out to the blubbering child and tell him that it was okay; that everything was all right. But it wasn't all right, might not ever be.

'Stop cryin' now, son. Stop cryin' an' tell me about it.'

''Bout what?' Darryl said, his words vibrating like a humming-bird's wings.

''Bout who you killed, that's what.'

'I ain't killed nobody,' Darryl said in a monotone.

'Yes you did. Either that or you saw sumpin'. I heard it in your deny when you didn't know I was talkin' 'bout Billy. I know when a man is guilty, Darryl. I know that down in my soul.'

Darryl looked away and set his mouth shut.

'I ain't a cop, li'l brother. I ain't gonna turn you in. But you kilt my friend out there an' we just et him down. I owe t'Billy an' to you too. So tell me about it. You tell me an' then you could go.'

They stared at each other for a long time.

10

Socrates grinned to put the boy at ease but he didn't look benevolent. He looked hungry.

Darryl felt like the meal.

4

He didn't want to say it but he didn't feel bad either. Why should he feel bad? It wasn't even his idea. Wasn't anybody's plan. It was just him and Jamal and Norris out in the oil fields above Baldwin Hills. Sometimes dudes went there with their old ladies. And if you were fast enough you could see some pussy and then get away with their pants.

They also said that the army was once up there and that there were old bullets and even hand grenades just lying around to be found.

But then this retarded boy showed up. He said he was with his brother but that his brother left him and now he wanted to be friends with Darryl and his boys.

'At first we was just playin',' Darryl told Socrates. 'You know – pushin' 'im an' stuff.'

But when he kept on following them – when he squealed every time they saw somebody – they hit him and pushed him down. Norris even threw a rock at his head. But the retard kept on coming. He was running after them and crying that they had hurt him. He cried louder and louder. And when they hit him, to shut him up, he yelled so loud that it made them scared right inside their chests.

'You know I always practice with my knife,'

Darryl said. 'You know you got to be able to get it out quick if somebody on you.'

Socrates nodded. He still practiced himself.

'I'ont know how it got in my hand. I swear I didn't mean t'cut 'im.'

'You kill'im?' Socrates asked.

Darryl couldn't talk but he opened his mouth and nodded.

They all swore never to tell anybody. They would kill the one who told about it – they swore on blood and went home.

'Anybody find 'im?' Socrates asked.

'I'ont know.'

The red spider danced while the woman in red kept her arms folded and stared her disapproval of all men – especially those two men. Darryl had to go to the bathroom. He had the runs after that big meal – and, Socrates thought, from telling his tale.

When he came out he looked ashy, his lips were ashen.

He slumped back in Socrates' cheap chair – drowsy but not tired. He was sick and forlorn.

For a long time they just sat there. The minutes went by but there was no clock to measure them. Socrates learned how to do without a timepiece in prison.

He counted the time while Darryl sat hopelessly by.

'What you gonna do, li'l brother?'

'What?'

'How you gonna make it right?'

'Make what right? He dead. I cain't raise him back here.'

When Socrates stared at the boy there was no telling what he thought. But what he was thinking didn't matter. Darryl looked away and back again. He shifted in his chair. Licked his dry lips.

'What?' he asked at last.

'You murdered a poor boy couldn't stand up to you. You killed your little brother an' he wasn't no threat; an' he didn't have no money that you couldn't take wit'out killin' 'im. You did wrong, Darryl. You did wrong.'

'How the fuck you know?' Darryl yelled. He would have said more but Socrates raised his hand, not in violence but to point out the truth to his dinner guest.

Darryl went quiet and listened.

'I ain't your warden, li'l brother. I ain't gonna show you to no jail. I'm just talkin' to ya – one black man to another one. If you don't hear me there ain't nuthin' I could do.'

'So I could go now?'

'Yeah, you could go. I ain't yo' warden. I just ask you to tell me how you didn't do wrong. Tell me how a healthy boy ain't wrong when he kills his black brother who sick.'

Darryl stared at Socrates, at his eyes now – not his hands.

'You ain't gonna do nuthin'?'

'Boy is dead now. Rooster's dead too. We cain't change that. But you got to figure out where you stand.'

'I ain't goin' t'no fuckin' jail if that's what you mean.'

Socrates smiled. 'Shoo'. I don't blame you for that. Jail ain't gonna help a damn thing. Better shoot yo'self than go to jail.'

'I ain't gonna shoot myself neither. Uh-uh.'

'If you learn you wrong then maybe you get to be a man.'

'What's that s'posed t'mean?'

'Ain't nobody here, Darryl. Just you'n me. I'm sayin' that I think you was wrong for killin' that boy. I know you killed'im. I know you couldn't help it. But you was wrong anyway. An' if that's the truth, an' if you could say it, then maybe you'll learn sumpin'. Maybe you'll laugh in the morning sometimes again.'

Darryl stared at the red spider. She was still now. He didn't say anything, didn't move at all.

'We all got to be our own judge, li'l brother. 'Cause if you don't know when you wrong then yo' life ain't worf a damn.'

Darryl waited as long as he could. And then he asked, 'I could go?'

14

'You done et Billy. So I guess that much is through.'

'So it ain't wrong that I killed'im 'cause I et him?'

'It's still wrong. It's always gonna be wrong. But you know more now. You ain't gonna kill no more chickens,' Socrates said. Then he grunted out a harsh laugh. 'At least not around here.'

Darryl stood up. He watched Socrates to see what he'd do.

'Yo' momma cook at home, Darryl?'

'Sometimes. Not too much.'

'You come over here anytime an' I teach ya how t'cook. We eat pretty good too.'

'Uh-huh,' Darryl answered. He took a step away from his chair.

Socrates stayed seated on his trash can.

Darryl made it all the way to the door. He grabbed the wire handle that took the place of a long-ago knob.

'What they put you in jail for?' Darryl asked.

'I killed a man an' raped his woman.'

'White man?'

'No.'

'Well . . . bye.'

'See ya, li'l brother.'

'I'm sorry . . . 'bout yo' chicken.'

'Billy wasn't none'a mine. He belonged to a old lady 'cross the alley.'

'Well . . . bye.'

'Darryl.'

15

'Yeah.'

'If you get inta trouble you could come here. It don't matter what it is – you could come here to me.'

6

Socrates stared at the door a long time after the boy was gone; for hours. The night came on and the cool desert air of Los Angeles came in under the door and through the cracks in his small shack of an apartment.

A cricket was calling out for love from somewhere in the wall.

Socrates looked at the woman, sun shining on her head. Her red sun hat threw a hot crimson shadow across her face. There was no respite for her but she still stood defiant. He tried to remember what Theresa looked like but it had been too long now. All he had left was the picture of a painting – and that wasn't even her. All he had left from her were the words she never said. *You are dead to me, Socrates. Dead as that poor boy and that poor girl you killed.*

He wondered if Darryl would ever come back.

He hoped so.

Socrates went through the doorless doorway into his other room. He lay down on the couch and just before he was asleep he thought of how he'd wake up alone. The rooster was hoarse in his old age, his crow no more than a whisper.

But at least that motherfucker tried.

MIDNIGHT MEETING

1

'I think we should go over there right now an' an' an' an' shoot'im in his head,' Right said. He held up his paralyzed left hand and gestured, meaninglessly, with the atrophied knuckle of his point finger.

'We cain't do that, man,' Markham Peal whined. He grabbed at the collar of his T-shirt and pulled on it until it stretched down far enough to reveal his weak, yellow-hued chest.

Right Burke and Stony Wile were sitting on the floor with their backs against the wall in Socrates Fortlow's small living room. Howard Shakur and Markham perched themselves on the couch that doubled for Socrates' bed.

It was a poor man's room. The wallpaper had been pink at one time but now it was worn down to shopping-bag brown. The wood slats of the floor had buckled in places and separated. A tall man would have brushed the ceiling with the top of his head. On a windy day even the open-faced gas heater couldn't keep it warm.

There were no windows. Socrates' only neighbors were two burned-out furniture stores and an almost always empty street.

The first year Socrates lived there he sent the rent to H. Price Landers, Esq., who received his mail at an address on Olympic Boulevard. Somewhere in the second year the money orders started coming back marked: Return to Sender/No Forwarding Address.

H. Price Landers had died, Socrates thought, and all that he owned was, at least for a while, forgotten.

'We ain't even sure that he did it, Right,' Stony Wile, the squat ship welder from East St Louis, said. 'It's just hearsay we goin' on.'

'Noooo, no.' No-neck Howard shook his head. He was both the heaviest and the youngest man in the room. 'My li'l girl ain't lyin'. She seen what I told ya. She saw Petis jump up on LeRoy with a knife. She told me that even 'fore they fount'im. If she saw LeRoy get it then you know she seen who give it to 'im.'

'She could be wrong,' Stony replied. 'It was nighttime. It was late. Lotsa men the same build as Petis.'

'She knew it were LeRoy. She knew he was dead. How she gonna mark one man an' then miss the other?'

'It could happen,' Stony said.

'Well if she saw it then let her go tell the cops. Cops the ones should take down a man if he did wrong. Ain't us who should do it.' Markham was wringing his T-shirt. Sweat formed on his forehead but it wasn't hot in the room.

'I ain't sendin' my baby down to no cops. Uh-uh,' Howard said. He swiveled his big head around on his shoulders and opened his eyes wide.

From somewhere blocks away four shots were fired in quick succession. The men all looked at the pinkish-brown wallpaper for a moment and then turned their attention back to the room.

'What you say, Socco?' Stony asked.

Their host was standing in the doorless doorway that led from the living room to the kitchen. He was listening to his friends and neighbors but somehow felt removed. Their talk about Petis and his crime had brought back memories of another man back in an Indiana jail.

'Socrates.'

'Yeah?'

'What you think about this shit here?'

Socrates squinted, then he rubbed his eyes with his big hands. He looked at Howard. Howard didn't have much of a neck but he was so fat that he had three chins to make up for it.

Howard didn't like the attention. He glared back at Socrates.

'What else Winnie see?' Socrates asked at last.

'What you mean?' Howard asked.

'I mean, did they fight? Did LeRoy say sumpin' to Petis? Why he gonna stab a man fo' nuthin'?'

'He robbin' 'im, Socco. You know that.'

'No I don't. I don't know it unless that's what you tellin' me. Did Winnie say Petis was robbin' 'im?'

'Yeah.' Howard moved his big shoulders around and shifted on the couch. 'He pult out the knife an' grabbed LeRoy by his shirt an' told him t'give up his money. When LeRoy said no, Petis stabbed him in the neck an' then tore out his pants pockets t'get what he had.'

'That's what Winnie said? You sure she didn't hear you an' Corina talkin' 'bout it after you read it?'

'Yeah. I'm sure. I told you that Winnie come to me first.'

The loud noise of a police helicopter sounded overhead. Socrates could feel the breeze from the rotors come in through the poorly insulated roof and walls. The helicopter hovered over the building for a minute or two before moving off.

'C-c-cops always be flyin',' Right said. 'Shit. If they come down here to earth sometimes maybe Petis wouldn't be goin' all over killin' folks for laundry money.'

Socrates was still staring at Howard.

'What?' Howard wanted to know. 'What you lookin' at?'

'What you want us to do, Howard?' Socrates asked.

'I got to go soon, boys,' Markham said. His collar was destroyed.

21

No one heeded him though. They were all looking at Howard.

'I don't know. Winnie come in an' told me what she seen. She was scared an' I thought I should do sumpin'. You know Petis prob'ly the one kilt all them people 'round here. Least all them's been stabbed. At least I wanted t'tell somebody.'

'Tell the cops,' Markham said.

'I got a pistol in my night table drawer got his name on the barrel.' Right Burke was the oldest among them – in his seventies. He'd been a combat soldier in World War Two. The left side of his body had been paralyzed by a stroke in '84. Since then he lived at Luvia's – she ran a kind of private retirement home in the neighborhood.

'Maybe we should just tell ev'rybody about it,' Stony said. 'Maybe then it'll just take care of itself.'

'Even I know that ain't gonna help,' cowardly Markham said.

The other men grumbled their agreement.

'What you think we should do?' Right asked Socrates. 'You the one know about people like Petis. You think if we told ev'rybody that that would stop him?'

'Dopehead?' Socrates sneered. 'No.'

'You think Howard should take Winnie an' go to the police?'

Socrates shook his head. 'Uh-uh. All Petis need is a first-year lawyer to have that baby girl's testimony th'owed out. He wouldn't even get to tiral 'less they got hard evidence. He be on the street in less than a week.'

'An' be knockin' on my do',' Howard added.

'Maybe not, Howard,' Socrates said. 'Dopehead don't usually carry a grudge. He too busy lookin' fo' his fix.'

'Well, anyway, I ain't gonna make my baby go through that. I ain't gonna mark her fo' that crazy man.'

'Kill 'im,' Right said again.

Markham farted.

Stony lit a match and blew it out to cover the smell.

Socrates felt how small his room was with all those men in it. Twenty-seven years in an Indiana prison had prepared him for the poverty he lived in. But he wished that he had a bigger room.

Maybe it was time to move.

'It's a hard choice, boys,' Socrates said. 'If it is Petis been robbin' an' killin' 'round here you could bet he gonna keep on doin' it. He got the taste'a blood now. It comes easy too 'im. You cain't talk to 'im, warn 'im, wound 'im, or turn him in to the cops.'

'Like I said.' Right let his statement hang in the air.

'I don't know about that, Brother Right,' Socrates said. 'We might be cornered, but we're not animals – not yet.'

'So you sayin' t'let it lie?' Right asked.

★   ★   ★

Socrates tried to think of an answer to Right's question. It wasn't the first time that he'd had such a problem.

He'd been thinking about Fitzroy ever since Howard and his friends had come over. When they told him about Petis he knew what they wanted.

They wanted him to kill Petis. After all, he was the one among them that had gone to prison for double murder. He knew how to do it.

Just like with Fitzroy.

Crazy Fitzroy who swore he had killed a man and woman from every race on the face of the earth. Fitzroy who raped you to show that he was boss; and broke your bones just to hear them snap.

The head warden gave Clyde Brown to Fitzroy for a cellmate as a kind of reward for keeping the other inmates down.

Clyde was the best cat burglar in the state. He came into prison cocksure and ready to play his time. Warden Johns decided, no one knew why, to make it his special province to break Clyde down.

And so Fitzroy.

In two weeks Clyde had lost his looks; he'd gone gaunt and thin. Bruises and blood married the boy's frightened face. He developed a twitch and would yell out loud at odd times for no reason at all.

Fitzroy's cell was never locked and so one night Clyde escaped. Socrates saw Clyde go by his cell in a shuffling sort of run. The boy was crying and looking behind him with the fear of death.

Fitzroy came on a few minutes later, smiling and walking fast.

The yell from Clyde that tore through the prison was enough to chill even Socrates' hot blood.

Socrates was no angel. He had brutalized men. But what Fitzroy did was different . . .

Or maybe, Socrates thought many years later in that room with his four friends, he wasn't so different.

The next night Socrates jammed the locking mechanism in his cell door. He stuck in a tin fork that made a sound like the lock catching. After the cell lights went out Socrates shoved his door free and walked out into the aisle.

He approached Fitzroy's cell with no mind at all. All he knew was that he had to stop what was going on. All he knew was that he couldn't live in his cell with what was happening down the hall.

Clyde, completely naked, had wedged himself between the toilet and the wall. Socrates didn't know if it was because he was trying to hide or if Fitzroy liked to keep him there.

Fitzroy lay back on his bunk, naked to the waist.

If Socrates' thinking mind had been working at that moment he would have known why men were afraid of Fitzroy. The man was a giant. Big arms, big chest, and a big stomach that seemed to be stretched over a solid oaken barrel.

He had big hands too, but Socrates' hands were larger.

Fitzroy lifted his head and focused his mud-colored eyes on the intruder. A smile came to his ragged lips. Even the scars on his face seemed to grin.

Now Socrates had a new thought in his mind. *If he gets to his feet I'm dead.*

By the time Fitzroy was sitting up Socrates was there over him. Before he could say a word Socrates struck with both fists in rapid order. The rock breakers, those hands were called.

Clyde grinned when he heard the muffled snap of vertebrae.

'I'm sayin',' Socrates said, looking the old veteran in the eye, 'that killin' ain't no answer for civilized men. I'm sayin' that bein' right won't wash the blood from your hands.'

The men listened. Stony even nodded.

'So they ain't nuthin' t'do, right?' Markham asked.

'I thought you said that you had somewhere t'be, Markham?' Socrates said in a friendly tone.

'Uh, well, I thought well, you know . . .'

'You could go on, brother.' Socrates stepped aside to make a way through the door. 'We could play some checkers next week.'

'Yeah,' Right said derisively. 'Go on.'

'Well, you know, my wife 'spects me home sometimes.'

Nobody spoke as Markham pushed himself up from the cushions. They were quiet as he pulled on his sweater and looked around the couch to make sure that nothing had fallen out of his pockets.

Markham tripped going through the doorway to the kitchen. Nobody said anything; nobody moved to see if he was okay.

No one spoke until they heard the door to the outside slam shut.

2

'Shit,' Right said. 'Fuckin' coward need t'run home t'his woman. Maybe he should sen' her down here.'

'I'ont know, man.' Stony coughed and ran his hand over his thick salt-and-pepper hair. 'Markham mighta been right. What could we do about dope addicts an' killers?'

'Yeah,' Socrates said. 'At least Markham know what he can do, an' what he cain't. That's all I ever ask of a man: tell me where you stand. That's all. You tell me where you stand an' then I know where I'm comin' from.'

Right and Stony nodded their agreement. Howard just sat there; distrust and fear in his eyes.

''Cause we don't want nobody cain't stand up to what's got to be done,' Socrates said.

'An' just what is that?' Howard asked.

'What's the biggest problem a black man have?' Socrates asked as if the answer was as plain as his wallpaper.

27

'A black woman,' Right said.

They all laughed – even Socrates.

'The po-lice,' said Howard.

Socrates smiled. 'Yeah, yeah. It's always trouble on the street – and at home too. But they ain't the problem – not really.'

'So what is?' Stony asked.

'Bein' a man, that's what. Standin' up an' sayin' what it is we want an' what it is we ain't gonna take.'

'Say to who?' Right asked. 'To the cops?'

'I don't believe in goin' t'no cops ovah somethin' like this here,' Socrates said. 'A black man – no matter how bad he is – bein' brutalized by the cops is a hurt to all of us. Goin' to the cops ovah a brother is like askin' for chains.'

'Uh-huh.' Stony was frowning, trying to understand. 'Then who we talk to? If not the cops, then a minister?'

Socrates just stared.

'I know,' Howard said.

'What?' asked Stony.

'He wanna go up to Petis. He wanna talk to him.'

Socrates smiled like a teacher approving of his student's lesson.

'Naw,' Right said. 'How talkin' to a killer gonna help?'

'He the one we mad at,' Howard answered. 'He the one done it. That's just it. Go up to the motherfucker an' tell'im we know who he is. Tell 'im that we ain't gonna take that shit. Tell'im what you said, Right. Tell'im that he's just hangin' by a thread.'

'You wit' me?' Socrates asked the men.

No one said no.

3

Socrates and his friends went to see Petis the next afternoon. They came to the last door on the left-hand side of the Magnolia Terrace, a horseshoe shaped court of cheap bungalow apartments. When they got there Socrates turned to his companions and said, 'Let me do the talkin'.'

Then he knocked and waited.

He knocked again.

A group of seven small children cruised by on plastic tricycles. They made squealing noises with their mouths and turned away down the cracked cement lane that the fourteen bungalows faced.

The thought of children near the dope fiend steeled Socrates.

'Who is it?' a voice called from behind the door.

'Me, Petis. Socrates Fortlow.'

'What you want, man?' the husky voice whined. 'I'm sleepin' in here.'

'I got money on my mind, Petis,' Socrates said. 'Money an' how you'n me could get some.'

Stony shifted from one foot to the other.

Right rubbed his nose with the back of his paralyzed hand.

The door came open and the men behind Socrates squared off. Petis stood there dressed only in a white T-shirt and blue boxer shorts.

Petis had the doorknob in his left hand, a six-inch carving knife in his right. He took a moment too long deciding whether to slam or to stab. In that moment of indecision Socrates delivered a terrible uppercut to the young man's gut.

The wind forced out of Petis smelled like the breath of a corpse. The tallish, loose-skinned man hurtled backwards and landed on the floor. Socrates walked in quickly and kicked the knife away.

A teenaged girl came running out of a closet. She was brown with small bare breasts and tight black panty hose. She looked at Socrates as if maybe he was there for her.

'Get your clothes on, girl,' Socrates said. 'An' get yo' ass outta here.'

Petis was vomiting on the floor.

'I thought you said that you just wanted to talk to'im,' Howard whispered in Socrates' ear.

'This is talk, Howard. It's the way to get a tough boy like Petis to pay attention.'

'You from my daddy?' the girl asked Socrates. She had pulled a short dress on over her head.

He regarded her for a long moment.

'Yeah. Yeah, that's right,' he said at last. 'Now get yo' ass home.'

'What you gonna do to Petty?'

'Talk to'im is all.'

That seemed to be enough for her. She grabbed a sack purse from out of the closet and made it through the group of men to the door.

'Close it,' Socrates said after she was gone.

It was dark in the room, with only a few shafts of light making it through the drawn and battered venetian blinds. Petis had stopped throwing up but he was still gasping after his breath.

One of the men flipped the light switch. The bare bulb from the overhead fixture could hardly have been called light.

When Socrates took a step back from Petis he noticed that the floor was sticky. He saw the bottle lying on its side. Somebody had spilled an orange soda and hadn't cleaned up.

The room was no larger than Socrates' living room. The only furniture was a straightback wooden chair and slender blue-and-white-striped mattress. Socrates pulled Petis up by an arm and put him in the chair.

Petis was young but his skin was old; gray instead of brown, loose and pocked. His eyes were dark but otherwise colorless.

'We know what you been doin', Petis,' Socrates said.

'What?'

Socrates slapped the young man so hard that he fell.

'Get back up in the chair, boy.'

'I . . .'

'Don't talk, Petis. Nobody wanna hear what you

31

got to say. We come here to talk to you. What you got to do is listen.'

While Petis reseated himself he looked around for an escape. When he saw that there was none he gave his attention to his bald accuser.

'We know what you been doin', Petis. We got a witness to you killin' LeRoy. We had a trial too . . .'

Socrates paused and grinned his most evil grin.

Petis belched and grabbed his stomach with both hands.

'One man wanted just to shoot you. One man wanted to go to the po-lice. We probably should kill you, I know. But finally we decided on sumpin' else.'

'What?' Petis asked quietly so that he wouldn't be hit again.

'You got to go, boy.'

'What you sayin'?'

'You got to go. Get outta here. Get outta this whole neighborhood. You got to go or else we kill you.'

'I ain't done nuthin',' Petis said.

Socrates slapped him.

'I ain't!' Petis sobbed loudly.

Socrates hit him again.

'You got to be gone by six, Petis. Six or we come in here and cut yo' th'oat wit' yo' own knife.' Socrates picked up the blade and shoved it in his belt.

'Six?'

Socrates slapped him one more time. 'Now what'd I say?'

'Okay, man. Okay. But I got to say goodbye to my mother first.'

'I don't think you understand – if I see you anywhere but on a bus outta Watts I'm gonna kill you. Kill you.

'There's twelve men behind me on this, junkie. Us four and another eight from our group. We gonna kill you if we see you. An' yo' momma ain't gonna stop that.'

Petis had begun to shake. Socrates stood there a good long while staring. He hated Petis. Hated him.

After a while he turned and said, 'Com'on. Let's go.'

They waited on the street opposite the courts, next to Howard's Buick. When Petis came out and saw them he ran back into his apartment.

At sunset Socrates sent his friends home.

'What you gonna do, Socco?' Right asked.

'Go on home to Luvia, Right. All'a you go on.' Just before seven he saw Petis's fleet shadow go toward the back of the courts. Before Socrates could react, the crackhead disappeared.

The apartment was empty. Socrates couldn't tell if Petis had gone for good or not because there was no telling what he might have taken or left behind.

So Socrates waited the night. He sat in the

33

dark and thought about poor Clyde. The warden had Clyde transferred to a hospital for the criminally insane. He was still there even while Socrates sat in the dark, the knife haft in his grip.

Petis didn't show up. Nobody heard about him for over a month. And when there was news it was about his death.

Petis had drifted downtown after that day. He didn't have any place to live and he was afraid to come back.

He begged and lived in alleys downtown. He robbed other street people and tried his hand at drug dealing – but failed.

Finally he got into a fight with a man he thought he could rob. Petis hadn't realized how weak he'd become. He never recovered from the beating.

Socrates watched his mother crying at the service.

4

'Maybe we should have us a regular group meetin' 'bout problems like Petis,' Stony said to Socrates one day as they were playing chess in South Park. 'It worked out good the first time.'

'I'ont think so, Stony. No I don't.'

'Why not?'

'We ain't some kinda gangbangers, man. We cain't live like that. We did what we had to do. But you know, I don't know if I'd have the heart ever to do it again.'

THE THIEF

1

Iula's grill sat on aluminum stilts above an open-air, fenced-in auto garage on Slauson. Socrates liked to go to the diner at least once a month on a Tuesday because they served meat loaf and mustard greens on Tuesdays at Iula's. The garage was run by Tony LaPort, who had rented the diner out to Iula since before their marriage; it was a good arrangement for Tony so he still leased to her eight years after their divorce.

Tony had constructed the restaurant when he was in love and so it was well built. The diner was made from two large yellow school buses that Tony had welded together – side by side. One bus held the counter where the customers sat, while the other one held the kitchen and storage areas. The banistered stairway that led up to the door was aluminum also. When Iula closed for the night she used a motor-driven hoist to lift the staircase far up off the street. Then she'd go through the trapdoor down a wooden ladder to Tony's work space, let herself out through the wire gate, and

36

set the heavy padlocks that Tony used to keep thieves out.

If the locks failed to deter an enterprising crook there was still Tina to contend with. Tina was a hundred-pound mastiff who hated everybody in the world except Iula and Tony. Tina sat right by the gate all night long, paws crossed in a holy prayer that some fool might want to test her teeth.

She was waiting that afternoon as Socrates approached the aluminum stairs. She growled in a low tone and Socrates found himself wondering if he would have a chance to crush the big dog's windpipe before she could tear out his throat. It was an idle thought; the kind of question that men discussed when they were in prison. In prison, studying for survival was the only real pastime.

How many ways were there to kill a man? What was more dangerous in a close fight – a gun or a knife? How long could you hold your breath underwater if there were policemen looking for you on the shore? Will God really forgive any sin?

Thinking about killing that dog was just habit for Socrates. The habit of twenty-seven years behind bars out of fifty-eight.

As he climbed the aluminum staircase he thought again about how well built it was. He liked the solid feeling that the light metal gave. He was happy because he could smell the mustard greens.

He could almost taste that meat loaf.

2

'Shet that do'!' Iula shouted, her back turned to Socrates. 'Damn flies like t'eat me up in here.'

'Shouldn't cook so damn good you don't want no notice, I.' Socrates slammed shut the makeshift screen door and walked up the stepwell into the bus.

The diner was still empty at four-thirty. Socrates came early because he liked eating alone. He went to the stool nearest Iula and sat down. The musical jangle of coins came from the pockets of his army jacket.

'You been collectin' cans again?' Iula had turned around to admire her customer. Her face was a deep amber color splattered with dark freckles, especially around her nose. She was wide-hipped and large-breasted. Three gold teeth decorated her smile. And she was smiling at Socrates. She put a fist on one hip and pushed her apron out, making an arc that brushed her side of the counter.

Socrates was looking at her breasts. Tony had once told him that the first time he saw those titties they were standing straight up, nipples pointing left and right.

'Yeah, I,' he said, in answer to her question. 'I got me a route now. Got three barmen keep the bottles an' cans on the side for me. All I gotta do is clean up outside for them twice a week. I made seventeen dollars just today.'

'Ain't none these young boys out here try an' take them bottles from you, Mr Fortlow?'

'Naw. Gangbanger be ashamed t'take bottles in a sto'. An' you know as long as I got my black jeans and khaki I don't got no color t'get them young bulls mad. If you know how t'handle them they leave you alone.'

'I'ont care what you say,' Iula said. 'Them boys make me sick wit' all that rap shit they playin' an' them guns an' drugs.'

'I seen worse,' Socrates said. 'You know these three men live in a alley off'a Crenshaw jump me today right after I got my can money.'

'They did?'

'Uh-huh. Fools thought they could take me.' Socrates held out his big black hand. The thick fingers were the size of large cigars. When he made a fist the knuckles rode high like four deadly fins.

Iula was impressed.

'They hurt you?' she asked.

Socrates looked down at his left forearm. There, near the wrist, was a sewn-up tear and a dark stain.

'What's that?' Iula cried.

'One fool had a bottle edge. Huh! He won't try an' cut me soon again.'

'Did he break the skin?'

'Not too much.'

'You been to a doctor, Mr Fortlow?'

'Naw. I went home an' cleaned it out. Then I sewed up my damn coat. I cracked that boy's arm 'cause he done ripped my damn coat.'

39

'You better get down to the emergency room,' Iula said. 'That could get infected.'

'I cleaned it good.'

'But you could get lockjaw.'

'Not me. In the penitentiary they gave you a tetanus booster every year. You might get a broke jaw in jail but you ain't never gonna get no lockjaw.'

Socrates laughed and set his elbows on the counter. He cleared his throat and looked at Iula watching him. Behind her was the kitchen and a long frying grill. There were big pots of beef and tomato soup, mashed potatoes, braised short ribs, stewed chicken, and mustard greens simmering on the stove. The meat loaves, Socrates knew from experience, were in bread pans in the heating pantry above the ovens.

It was hot in Iula's diner.

Hotter under her stare.

She put her hand on Socrates' arm.

'You shouldn't be out there hustlin' bottles, Mr. Fortlow,' she said. Her voice was like the rustling of coarse blankets.

'I got t'eat. An' you know jobs don't grow on trees, I. Anyway, I got a bad temper. I might turn around one day and break a boss man's nose.'

Iula laid her finger across his knucklebones.

'You could work here,' she said. 'There's room enough for two behind this here counter.'

Iula turned her head to indicate what she meant.

40

In doing so she revealed her amber throat. It was a lighter shade than her face.

He remembered another woman, just a girl really, and her delicate neck. That woman died by the same hand Iula stroked. She died and hadn't done a thing to deserve even a bruise. He had killed her and was a little sorrier every day; every day for thirty-five years. He got sadder but she was still dead. She was dead and he was still asking himself why.

'I don't know,' he said.

'What?'

'I don't know what to say, I.'

'What is there to say?' she demanded. 'All you could say is yeah. You ain't got hardly a dime. You need a job. And the Lord knows I could use you too.'

'I got to think about it,' he said.

'Think about it?' Just that fast Iula was enraged. 'Think about it? Here I am offerin' you a way outta that hole you in. Here I am offerin' you a life. An' you got to think about it? Look out here in the streets around you, Mr. Fortlow. Ain't no choice out there. Ain't nuthin' t'think about out there.'

Socrates didn't have to look around to see the boarded-up businesses and stores; the poor black faces and brown faces of the men and women who didn't have a thing. Iula's diner and Tony's garage were the only working businesses on that block.

And he hated bringing bottles and cans to the Ralph's supermarket on Crenshaw. To get there

41

he had to walk for miles pulling as many as three grocery carts linked by twisted wire coat hangers. And when he got there they always made him wait; made him stand outside while they told jokes and had coffee breaks. And then they checked every can. They didn't have to do that. He knew what they took and what they didn't. He came in twice a week with his cans and bottles and nobody ever found one Kessler's Root Beer or Bubble-Up in the lot. But they checked every one just the same. And they never bothered to learn his name. They called him 'Pop' or 'old man'. They made him wait and checked after him like he was some kind of stupid animal.

But he took it. He took it because of that young girl's neck; because of her boyfriend's dead eyes. Those young people in Ralph's were stupid and arrogant and mean – but he was evil. That's what Socrates thought.

That's what he believed.

'Well?' Iula asked.

'I'd . . . I'd like some meat loaf, Iula. Some meat loaf with mashed potatoes and greens.'

From the back of her throat Iula hissed, 'Damn you!'

3

Socrates felt low but that didn't affect his appetite. He'd learned when he was a boy that the next meal was never a promise; only a fool didn't eat when he could.

He laced his mashed potatoes and meat loaf with pepper sauce and downed the mustard greens in big noisy mouthfuls. When he was finished he looked behind the counter hoping to catch Iula's eye. Iula would usually give Socrates seconds while smiling and complimenting him on the good appetite he had.

'You eat good but you don't let it turn to fat,' she'd say, admiring his big muscles.

But now she was mad at him for insulting her offer. Why should she feed the kitty when there wasn't a chance to win the pot?

'I,' Socrates said.

'What you want?' It was more a dare than a question.

'Just some coffee, babe,' he said.

Iula slammed the mug down and flung the Pyrex coffeepot so recklessly that she spilled half of what she poured. But Socrates didn't mind. He was still hungry and so finished filling the mug with milk from two small serving pitchers on the counter.

He had eleven quarters in his right-hand jacket pocket. Two dollars and fifty cents for the dinner and twenty-five cents more for Iula's tip. That was a lot of money when all you had to your name was sixty-eight quarters, four dimes, three nickels, and eight pennies. It was a lot of money but Socrates was still hungry – and that meat loaf smelled better than ever.

Iula used sage in her meat loaf. He couldn't make it himself because all he had at home was a hot plate and you can't make meat loaf on a hot plate.

'Iula!'

Socrates turned to see the slim young man come up into the bus. He was wearing an electric-blue exercise suit, zipped up to the neck, and a bright yellow headband.

'Wilfred.' There were still no seconds in Iula's voice.

'How things goin'?' the young man asked.

'Pretty good if you don't count for half of it.'

'Uh-huh,' he answered, not having heard. 'An' where's Tony today?'

'It's Tuesday, ain't it?'

'Yeah.'

'Then Tony's down at Christ Congregational settin' up for bingo.'

Wilfred sat himself at the end of the counter, five stools away from Socrates. He caught the older man's eye and nodded – as black men do.

Then he said, 'I done built me up a powerful hunger today, Iula. I got two hollow legs to fill.'

'What you want?' she asked, not at all interested in the story he was obviously wanting to tell.

'You got a steak back there in the box?'

'Shit.' She would have spit on the floor if she wasn't in her own restaurant.

'Okay. Okay. I tell you what. I want some stewed

chicken, some braised ribs, an' two thick slabs'a meat loaf on one big plate.'

'That ain't on the menu.'

'Charge me a dinner for each one then.'

Iula's angry look changed to wonder. 'You only get one slice of meat loaf with a dinner.'

'Then ring it up twice, honey. I got mad money for this here meal.'

Iula stared until Wilfred pulled out a fan of twenty-dollar bills from his pocket. He waved the fan at her and said, 'Don't put no vegetables on that shit. You know I'm a workin' man – I needs my strength. I need meat.'

Iula moved back into the kitchen to fill Wilfred's order.

Socrates sipped his coffee.

'Hey, brother,' Wilfred said.

Socrates looked up at him.

'How you doin'?' the young man offered.

'Okay, I guess.'

'You guess?'

'It depends.'

'Depends on what?'

'On what comes next.'

When Wilfred smiled, Socrates could see that he was missing one of his front teeth.

'You jus' livin' minute t'minute, huh?' the young man said.

'That's about it.'

'I used to be like that. Used to be. That is till I fount me a good job.' Wilfred sat back as well as

45

he could on the stool and stared at Socrates as if expecting to be asked a question.

Socrates took another sip of coffee. He was thinking about another helping of meat loaf and his quarters, about Iula's nipples, and that long-ago dead girl. He didn't have any room for what was on the young man's mind.

Iula came out then with a platter loaded down with meats. It was a steaming plate looking like something out of the dreams Socrates had had when he was deep inside of his jail sentence.

'Put it over there, Iula.' Wilfred was pointing to the place next to Socrates. He got up from his stool and went to sit behind the platter.

He was a tall man, in his twenties. He'd shaved that morning and had razor bumps along his jaw and throat. His clothes were bulky and Socrates wondered why. He was thin and well built. Obviously from *the hood* – Socrates could tell that from the hunger he brought to his meal.

'What's your name, man?' Wilfred asked.

'Socrates.'

'Socrates? Where'd you get a name like that?'

'We was poor and country. My mother couldn't afford school so she figured that if she named me after somebody smart then maybe I'd get smart.'

'I knew it was somebody famous. You see?' Wilfred said, full of pride. 'I ain't no fool. I know shit too. I got it up here. My name is Wilfred.'

Socrates breathed in deeply the smells from Wilfred's plate. He was still hungry – having walked a mile for every two dollars he'd made that day.

His stomach growled like an angry dog.

'What you eatin', Socco?' Wilfred asked. Before giving him a chance to answer he called out to Iula, 'What's my brother eatin', Iula? Bring whatever it is out to 'im. I pay for that too.'

While Iula put together Socrates's second plate, Wilfred picked up a rib and sucked the meat from the bone.

He grinned and said, 'Only a black woman could cook like this.'

Socrates didn't know about that but he was happy to see the plate Iula put before him.

4

Socrates didn't pick up his fork right away. Instead he regarded his young benefactor and said, 'Thank you.'

'That's okay, brother. Eat up.'

Halfway through his second meal Socrates' hunger eased a bit. Wilfred had demolished his four dinners and pushed his plate away.

'You got some yams back there?' he called out to Iula.

'Yeah,' she answered. She had gone to a chair in her kitchen to rest and smoke a cigarette before more customers came.

47

'Bring out a big plate for me an' my friend here.'

Iula brought out the food without saying a word to Socrates. But he wasn't worried about her silence.

He came around on Tuesdays, when Tony was gone, because he wanted Iula for something; a girlfriend, a few nights in bed, maybe more, maybe. He hadn't touched a woman since before prison.

And now he was afraid of what his hands could do.

Iula was petulant but she didn't understand how scared he was even to want her.

She wanted a man up there on stilts with her to lift tubs of shortening that she couldn't budge. She wanted a man to sit down next to her in the heat that those stoves threw off.

If he came up there he'd probably get fat.

'What you thinkin' about, brother?' Wilfred asked.

'That they ain't nuthin' for free.'

'Well . . . maybe sometime they is.'

'Maybe,' Socrates said. 'But I don't think so.'

Wilfred grinned.

Socrates asked, 'What kinda work you do, Wilfred?'

'I'm self-employed. I'm a businessman.'

'Oh yeah? What kinda business?'

Wilfred smiled and tried to look coy. 'What you think?'

'I'd say a thief,' Socrates answered. He speared a hot yam and pushed it in his mouth.

Wilfred's smile widened but his eyes went cold.

'You got sumpin' against a man makin' a livin'?' he asked.

'Depends.'

''Pends on what?'

'On if it's wrong or not.'

'Stealin's stealin', man. It's all the same thing. You got it – I take it.'

'If you say so.'

'That's what I do say,' Wilfred said. 'Stealin's right for the man takin' an' wrong fo' the man bein' took. That's all they is to it.'

Socrates decided that he didn't like Wilfred. But his stomach was full and he'd become playful. 'But if a man take some bread an' he's hungry, starvin',' he said. 'That's not wrong to nobody. That's good sense.'

'Yeah. You right,' Wilfred conceded. 'But s'pose you hungry for a good life. For a nice house with a bathtub an' not just some shower. S'pose you want some nice shoes an' socks don't bust out through the toe the first time you wear'em?'

'That depends too.'

''Pends on what? What I want don't depend on a damn thing.' Wilfred's smile was gone now.

'Maybe not. I mean maybe the wantin' don't depend on nuthin' but how you get it does, though.'

'Like what you mean?'

'Well let's say that there's a store sellin' this good life you so hungry for. They got it in a box somewhere. Now you go an' steal it. Well, I guess that's okay. That means the man got the good life give it up to you. That's cool.'

'Shit,' Wilfred said. 'If they had a good life in a box you know I steal me hunnert'a them things. I be right down here on Adams sellin' 'em for half price.'

'Uh-huh. But they don't have it in a box now do they?'

'What you tryin' t'say, man?' Wilfred was losing patience. He was, Socrates thought, a kind benefactor as long as he didn't have to see a man eye to eye.

'I'm sayin' that this good life you talkin' 'bout stealin' comes outta your own brother's house. Either you gonna steal from a man like me or you gonna steal from a shop where I do my business. An' ev'ry time I go in there I be payin' for security cameras an' security guards an' up-to-the-roof insurance that they got t'pay off what people been stealin'. An' they gonna raise the prices higher'n a motherfucker to pay the bills, wit' a little extra t'pay us back for you stealin'.'

Socrates thought that Wilfred might get mad. He half expected the youth to pull out a gun. But Socrates wasn't worried about a gun in those quarters. He was stronger than Wilfred, and, as he had learned in prison, a strong arm can beat a gun up close.

50

But Wilfred wasn't mad. He laughed happily. He patted Socrates on the shoulder, feeling his hard muscle, and said, 'You got a good tongue there, brother. You good as a preacher, or a cop, when it comes to talkin' that talk.'

Wilfred stood up and Socrates swiveled around on his seat, ready for the fight.

Iula sensed the tension and came out with a cigarette dangling from her lips.

Wilfred stripped off his exercise jacket and stepped out of the gaudy nylon pants. Underneath he was wearing a two-piece tweed suit with a brown suede vest. His silk tie showed golden-and-green clouds with little flecks of red floating here and there. His shirt was white as Sunday's clothesline.

'What you think?' Wilfred asked his audience.

Iula grunted and turned back to her kitchen. He was too skinny for her no matter what he had on.

'Come here,' Wilfred said to Socrates. 'Look out here in the street.'

Socrates went to the bus window and crouched down to look outside. There was a new tan car, a foreign job, parked out there. Socrates didn't know the model but it looked like a nice little car.

'That's my ride,' Wilfred said.

'Where it take you?' Socrates asked.

'Wherever I wanna go,' Wilfred answered. 'But mostly I hit the big malls an' shoppin' centers up in West Hollywood, Beverly Hills, Santa Monica, and what-have-you.

'I get one'a my girlfriends to rent me a car. Then

51

I get all dressed up like this an' put on a runnin' suit, or maybe some funky clothes like you got on, over that. An' I always got me a hat or a headband or somethin'. You know they could hardly ever pick you out of a lineup if you had sumpin' on yo' head.'

Socrates had learned that in jail too.

'I grab 'em in the parkin' lot.' Wilfred sneered with violent pleasure. 'I put my knife up hard against they necks an' tell'em they dead. You know I don't care if I cut 'em up a li'l bit. Shit. I had one young Jap girl peed on herself.'

Wilfred waited for a laugh or something. When it didn't come the jaunty young man went back to his seat.

'You don't like it,' Wilfred said. 'Too bad.'

'I don't give a damn what you do, boy,' Socrates answered. He sat back down and scooped up the last bit of gravy in his spoon. 'I cain't keep a fool from messin' up.'

'I ain't no fool, old man. I don't mess up neither. I get they money an' cut 'em up some so they call a doctor fo' they call the cops. Then I run an' th'ow off my niggah clothes. When the cops come I'm in my suit, in my car comin' home. An' if they stop me I look up all innocent an' lie an' tell'em that I work for A&M Records. I tell'em that I'm a manager in the mailroom over there. No sir, I don't fuck up at all.'

'Uh-huh,' Socrates said. He put a yam in his mouth after dipping it in the honey butter sauce at the bottom of the dish; it was just about the best thing he had ever tasted.

'Mothahfuckah, you gonna sit there an' dis me with yo' mouth fulla the food I'm buyin'?' Wilfred was amazed.

'You asked me an' I told ya,' Socrates said. 'I don't care what you do, boy. But that don't mean I got to call it right.'

'What you talkin' 'bout, man? I ain't stealin' from no brother. I ain't stealin' where no po' brother live. I'm takin' the good life from people who got it – just like you said.'

'You call my clothes funky, din't ya, boy?'

'Hey, man. I din't mean nuthin'.'

'Yes you did,' Socrates said. 'You think I'm funky an' smelly an' I ain't got no feelin's. That's what you think. You don't see that I keep my socks darned an' my clothes clean. You don't see that you walkin' all over me like I was some piece'a dog shit. An' you don't care. You just put on a monkey suit an' steal a few pennies from some po' woman's purse. You come down here slummin', flashin' your twenty-dollar bills, talkin' all big. But when you all through people gonna look at me like I'm shit. They scared'a me 'cause you out there pretendin' that you're me robbin' them.'

Wilfred held up his hands in a false gesture of surrender and laughed. 'You too deep for me, brother,' he said. He was smiling but alert to the violence in the older man's words. 'Way too deep.'

53

'You the one shovelin' it, man. You the one out there stealin' from the white man an' blamin' me. You the one wanna be like them in their clothes. You hatin' them an' dressed like the ones you hate. You don't even know who the hell you is!'

Socrates had to stop himself from striking Wilfred. He was shaking, scared of his own hands again.

'I know who I am all right, brother,' Wilfred said. 'And I'm a damn sight better'n you.'

'No you not,' Socrates said. A sense of calm came over him. 'No you not. You just dressin' good, eatin' like a pig. But when the bill come due I'm the one got t'pay it. Me an' all the rest out here.'

'All right, fine!' Wilfred shouted. 'But the only one right now payin' fo' somethin' is me. I'm the one got you that food you been eatin'. But if you don't like it then pay for it yourself.'

Iula came out again. Socrates noted the pot of steaming water she carried.

'I do you better than that, boy,' Socrates said. 'I'll pay for yo' four dinners too.'

'What?' Wilfred and Iula both said.

'All of it,' Socrates said. 'I'll pay for it all.'

'You a new fool, man,' Wilfred said.

Socrates stood up and then bent down to pick up Wilfred's stickup clothes from the floor.

'You always got to pay, Wilfred. But I'll take this bill. I'll leave the one out there for you.'

Wilfred faked a laugh and took the clothes from Socrates.

'Get outta here, man,' Socrates said.

For a moment death hung between the two men. Wilfred was full of violence and pride and Socrates was sick of violent and prideful men.

'I don't want no trouble in here now!' Iula shouted when she couldn't take the tension anymore.

Wilfred smiled again and nodded. 'You win, old man,' he said. 'But you crazy though.'

'Just get outta here,' Socrates said. 'Go.'

Wilfred considered for the final time doing something. He was probably faster than the older man. But it was a small space and strength canceled out speed in close quarters.

Socrates read all of that in Wilfred's eyes. Another young fool, he knew, who thought freedom was out the back door and in the dark.

Wilfred turned away slowly, went down the stairwell, then down the aluminum staircase to the street.

Socrates watched the tan car drive off.

5

'You're insane, Socrates Fortlow, you know that?' Iula said. She was standing on her side of the counter in front of seventeen stacks of four quarters each.

'You got to pay for your dinner, I.'

'But why you got to pay for him? He had money.'

'That was just a loan, I. But the interest was too much for me.'

'You ain't responsible fo' him.'

'You wrong there, baby. I'm payin' for niggahs like that ev'ry day. Just like his daddy paid for me.'

'You are a fool.'

'But I'm my own fool, I.'

'I don't get it,' she said. 'If you so upstandin' an' hardworkin' an' honest – then why don't you wanna come here an' work fo' me? Is it 'cause I'm a woman? 'Cause you don't wanna work fo' no woman?'

Socrates was feeling good. He had a full stomach. The muscles in his arms relaxed now that he didn't have to fight. There was an ache in his forearm where he'd been cut, but, as the prison doctor used to say, pain was just a symptom of life.

Socrates laughed.

'You're a woman all right, I. I know you had that boilin' water out there t'save me from Wilfred. You a woman all right, and I'm gonna be comin' back here every Tuesday from now on. I'm gonna come see you and we gonna talk too, Momma. Yeah. You gonna be seein' much more'a me.'

He got up and kissed her on the cheek before leaving. When his lips touched her skin a sound came from the back of her throat. Socrates heard that satisfied hum in his dreams every night for a month.

6

Socrates only had four dimes, three nickels, and eight pennies left to his name. If he took a bus he'd be broke, but he was just as happy to walk. On the way home he thought about finding a job somewhere. Some kind of work, he thought, where you didn't have to bleed and die for your meal.

DOUBLE STANDARD

1

It was an L.A. rain, straight down and hard. Socrates stood under the shelter of a glass bus stop. The walls had been smashed away but the roof was still intact. He stood in the gloomy twilight waiting for the RTD bus because there was a chill in his chest and three miles walking in the rain might have been his last walk.

Across the street two lovers stood under a doorway. At least she stood in the shelter of the small adobe ledge that jutted out over the abandoned shop's door. Socrates thought that the store was a baker's shop at one time because there was a faded sign that had wan blue and white checker squares across it; the letters HEL were all that was left of the word spelled out over the blue design.

A baker's shop, Socrates thought. He could see in his mind's eye the black men and women waking up at three a.m. and taking the same bus that he waited for to get there by four-thirty. He could almost feel the sleep in their eyes and the stiff yawns that came out when they tried to say good morning;

58

the shiver in their bones as they uncovered the big blending machines and the bitter taste of coffee on the back humps of their tongues. A pattern as regular as those blue and white checks. Each one a perfect little square, each one exactly the same size as the one before it – and the one after.

The paycheck had little blue and white squares on it, Socrates was sure. They made good money at the bakery, on the whole, because bakers worked long hours and long weeks.

Socrates was happy thinking about those prosperous black people. Hard workers making money, taking the bus to their little houses down on Central, sending their kids off to school.

He smiled and saw again the lovers wrestling in front of the boarded-up shop.

The man was large, verging on fat. His unprotected backside was getting soaked by the rain cascading off the ledge. But he didn't care at all. He hunched down over the small woman kissing and touching, pressing her hard against the door. She held on to his big neck with both hands, doing pull-ups to get to his lips in those few times that he reared back to look at her.

The violent rhythmless rain accompanied their passion. They lunged with their mouths, moved their hands like blind beggars hustling after a dropped coin.

'Ralphie,' she cried.

Socrates barely heard her over the din of rain.

Ralphie suddenly leaned back, taking her up

with him until she could wrap her legs around his waist. She was wearing a short skirt. Her legs were bare. If she had on any underwear Socrates couldn't make it out.

The young woman rested her head on Ralphie's shoulder and called out things into his ear.

For some reason it all seemed to fit. The rain, the lost business, the lovers out in the empty street in the failing light.

He turned away, giving them what privacy he could, and saw a bus coming down the avenue. He peered out intently, hoping that it was his bus – that he'd be home soon.

2

'Ralphie! Ralphie!' the young woman screamed.

Socrates stared harder at the bus.

'Ralphie! The bus, baby!' she cried.

The lovers came running across the street, splashing through puddles and squealing from the cold rain.

In the shelter of the bus stop she smoothed down her short skirt and pushed back her gold-frosted, straightened hair. Even though their eyes met she didn't really look at Socrates. Her smile was not for him. But he reveled in the glistening dark eyes and smug satisfaction that sang through her body.

Ralphie was trying to press his erection down to the side so that it wouldn't be seen pressing against his pants. When she put out her hand to help him he pushed it away and gave Socrates a shy sideways glance.

'It's the 86A,' she said, pointing at the bus.

Not Socrates' line.

'Why'ont you wait for the next one?' Ralphie asked. His voice was gruff and petulant at once.

The bus was only half a block away, barreling down fast.

'Come on, Linda,' Ralphie demanded. 'Stay.'

Even the way they talked was like sex; Ralphie begging for it and Linda . . . Linda wanted to give it to him but she couldn't. She had to get on that bus and so decided to enjoy the sweet pain she was bringing her man.

'I got to go, Ralphie,' she said, cold as that rain. 'I'll see you Tuesday though. Right?'

The bus's brakes squealed up to the stop.

'Stay,' he said, taking her by the hand.

The bus doors came open and Linda took a step backward into the door.

'Come on. Hurry it up,' the bus driver said.

Linda, both feet up in the bus and bent half over, tugged twice against Ralphie's grip. She yelled, 'Let me go, Ralphie!' like a child trying to get her best friend in trouble.

She couldn't have broken the big man's grip, his hands were almost as large as Socrates' rock-breaking mitts, but Ralphie let her go. She fell backwards into the bus. The doors levered shut immediately.

'See you Tuesday!' Ralphie cried out but the bus was already moving on.

The big man got on his tiptoes in a vain attempt to see her one last time. But the rain was too hard and the bus swerved at the wrong angle – even if the weather had been good he wouldn't have been able to see her.

Ralphie? Socrates thought.

3

Close up Socrates could see Ralphie's dark face. It protruded from his oval-shaped head. A perfect egg head with fish eyes and big sensual lips that, Socrates imagined, were even more swollen from Linda chewing on them. The big man didn't want to have anything to do with Socrates. That was no surprise. Socrates' khakis were stained and faded, there were thick veins at the knees from where he'd mended the secondhand pants. His bright, red-striped T-shirt, even under the army jacket, made him look like some kind of fool. Top all that off with a tan fishing cap that had *Fisherman's Wharf* stitched across it, and you had a bum – what people called a street person in the 1990s.

Socrates liked to talk to people, but he didn't have to talk to Ralphie. He didn't care about the young man. He would have let things lie if the bus had come; if the rain had let up and allowed him to wander away from the shelter; if Ralphie had just nodded or said something to make him feel like he was at least considered a part of the human race.

There was a time that Socrates would have hurt a man for ignoring him the way Ralphie did.

Socrates Fortlow was a violent man. He'd come up hard and gave as good as he got. The rage he carried brought him to prison but the Indiana Correctional Authority wasn't able to stem his anger.

He looked Ralphie in the eye, giving him one last chance to be civil. Ralphie registered no more recognition than if a stray dog had regarded him.

'Your backside got pretty wet there, brother,' Socrates said, proving that he had the ability to speak.

The young man looked. Then he sneered and shook his head.

'Listen, man.' Ralphie pointed his finger. 'I'm lettin' you stay here 'cause nobody should be out in no rain like this. But I don't want you talkin' t'me. Hear?'

Socrates smiled.

'What you laughin' at, niggah?' Ralphie wanted to know.

'Oh,' Socrates sang. 'I just think it's funny.'

'What's funny?' Ralphie took a step forward. Another man might have been frightened of Ralphie's bulk, but Socrates wasn't scared.

'I don't know. I mean, here you are callin' me a niggah an' really it's you the one playin' the niggah on yo' own wife an' kids. Here you are, out here pushin' up against some teenage girl, an' you got a perfectly good woman up at home.'

If a black man coulda turnt white you know Ralphie woulda been able to run for president right then. That's what Socrates said to Right Burke two weeks later.

Ralphie's eyes bulged and he seemed to lose his balance for a moment. He put out a hand to steady himself against the shelter, but the glass wall had been busted out long ago and the big man stumbled sideways.

Socrates grabbed him and helped him upright.

'What you talkin' 'bout, man?' Ralphie said, pushing the powerful hands away.

Socrates smiled again. 'You know what I'm sayin'. You Ralphie McPhee, right? Yes you are.'

'Who the fuck are you?' Ralphie demanded.

'What difference that make? Just before you wouldn't even say boo to me. Now you wanna be my friend?'

'Don't mess wit' me, old man. I might have to fuck you up.'

'Fuck wit' me an' you ain't never gonna fuck that li'l girl again,' Socrates said. He tried not to use foul language too much after prison but he knew that he had to get the point across to Ralphie before Ralphie made the mistake of trying to fight.

It worked.

Ralphie took a closer look at Socrates and saw something. Something that poor men living on the edge of mayhem can recognize without naming.

Socrates knew what he saw; the look of hard resolve. Socrates was ready for anything and he and Ralphie both knew it.

'Fuck you, man.' Ralphie took a step back from danger. 'Fuck you.'

'Uh-huh. Yeah. Tell me sumpin', Ralphie.' When no reply came, Socrates went on, 'How come you out here actin' like a niggah an' you cain't even see me?'

Ralphie wasn't listening. His eyes were roving over the possibilities of the problems he could have over being seen. 'Huh?' he snorted.

'I said, how come you out here actin' like a niggah?'

'What you talkin' 'bout, fool?'

'I'm sayin' that here you are out in these streets dry-humpin' some girl in front of a man live on'y two blocks from you. Shoot! I done talked to your wife an' yo' li'l boy, what's his name? Yeah. Warren.'

It was hearing his son's name that put real fear into Ralphie.

'Hey, man,' he said. 'This ain't none'a your fuckin' business.'

'It ain't?'

'Not one bit. So you just better shet yo' trap an' forget what you think you know. 'Cause you don't know a damn thing about me.'

'Oh yeah I do,' Socrates said. 'I know you. I know you front and back.'

'Hey!' Ralphie pushed his hands out and to the

side in a mock breaststroke. 'I'll kick holy shit outta you you wanna fuck wit' me!'

'Touch me.' Socrates pointed down at the dark cement under their feet. 'And I will leave you cold an' dead on this here flo'.'

Ralphie saw the hand slip into the khaki pocket, he saw the flat mud luster in the older man's eyes. He drew back into silence except for a hiccough that he couldn't stifle.

Just then a police car cruised slowly by. The two white faces peered through the glass and rain at the two black men. A light flashed out and the patrol car slowed almost to a stop – but then it went on.

The rain, Socrates thought. *Boys don't wanna get wet.*

4

'You gonna answer my question, boy?'

'What you want, man? You want a couple'a dollars?'

'I wanna know what you got against yo' wife, um, uh . . . Angel.'

Socrates saw the name sink into Ralphie's shoulders. The young man slumped down and shook his head.

'I'ont even know you, man,' Ralphie said.

'That's right. You cain't even see me when I'm standin' here right next to you. Cain't even say,

Hey, brother, what's happenin'. You cain't see me but I could see you.'

'So what do you want?'

It wasn't so much the question but the pain in Ralphie's voice that stopped Socrates cold. He thought about those imaginary workers in the bakery that might have stood there. He thought about thinking about what he'd do if they ever let him out of jail. He thought about the cold in his chest and the fact that the wiring in his apartment couldn't take the strain of an extra electric space heater.

A hundred needs went through Socrates' mind but nowhere could he find Ralphie. Maybe Linda. Maybe her bare brown legs wrapped around his waist. Maybe her.

'Yeah?' Ralphie demanded. 'You just gonna stand there an' look at the rain?'

Socrates considered the young man again. He wore black pants with a white shirt that had an off-white T-shirt showing at the open collar. His trench coat was drab green, darkened by the rain.

The shirt meant that he had a job in some store or office.

A workingman.

'Well?' Ralphie asked.

Socrates thought about a promise he'd made. A murky pledge. He swore to himself that he'd never hurt another person – except if he had to for self-preservation. He swore to try and do good

67

if the chance came before him. That way he could ease the evil deeds that he had perpetrated in the long evil life that he'd lived.

The sound of the rain filled the air and he got the urge to tear off his own ears.

'I'm sorry,' Socrates said.

'What?'

'I'm sorry,' he said again. He tried to remember the last time he'd apologized. He'd regretted the crimes of his youth; blubbered like a child over the couple he'd slaughtered. But they were dead. He had never, in his memory, apologized to a living soul.

'What the fuck is that's posed t'mean? You sorry?'

'I was just mad, that's all,' Socrates said. 'Mad that you an' yo' girlfriend din't even see me. Yeah, yeah. That's it.'

Ralphie was lost. He tried to stay angry but all that showed on his face was confusion. He didn't know whether to speak or to stand back.

Socrates saw a bus coming from many blocks away.

'You see,' Socrates said, 'I was talkin' about Angel and Warren. About how you was hurtin' them. But really it wasn't that. At least not just that.'

'How the fuck you know 'bout what I'm doin' t'my wife and son?' Ralphie said.

Socrates watched the bus coming over Ralphie's shoulder. He could make out the bright lights of the big windows up front. It was like a chariot burning in the rain.

'I don't mean to disrespect you, son,' Socrates said in a mild tone. 'It's just that you're only a little ways up the road from your own house. People who know you go up and down this street. If they see you an' that girl it's gonna hurt Angel an' you know they ain't no reason for that. Is there?'

The bus behind Ralphie stopped at a red light.

'She cain't be tellin' me what I could do an' what I cain't,' he said at last.

'Me neither, Ralphie. Me neither. You do what you got to, son. I just mean . . .' Socrates paused for a moment and wondered what it was exactly that he did mean. 'I'm just sayin' that we got to know what we doin'. Linda got sumpin' you need? Okay. But you don't have to rub Angel's nose in that. It's just like you did to me . . .'

'What I did to you?'

'You looked right through me, brother.' Socrates felt tears in his eyes. 'You across the street gettin' your nut offa that girl right in front'a me like I was some kinda animal, like I didn't even matter at all. An' then you couldn't even nod to me . . .'

The bus rolled up to the shelter.

It was their bus.

The brake sighed and the door levered open.

Ralphie moved toward the door.

Socrates fought the urge to grab the man's arm, to keep him there listening to his apologies.

But he didn't reach out. Ralphie got on the

bus. The doors slammed shut. And the bus glided away on a film of water that shimmered with street light.

5

'That's how I got sick,' Socrates told Right Burke from his foldout sofa bed. He'd been laid up with a bad chest cold for many days after he'd walked three miles in the rain. He'd been alone until Right Burke, a retired WWII veteran, came by to see where he'd been.

After seeing Socrates prostrate in the cold house, Right went out for aspirin and soup mix. He brought flavored gelatin and apple brandy to ward off the virus.

The first two days Socrates was too sick to say anything but what he absolutely had to. On the third day he thanked the maimed ex-sergeant and told him the story of Ralphie and Linda.

'I still don't see why you had to walk home in the rain,' Right said.

'I had to let'im go, Right. I had to let'im be.'

'You mean you was gonna kick his ass if you got on the bus together?'

'Uh-uh. Naw. I mean . . .' Socrates was lost for a moment, straining for breath on the thin mattress. 'I wasn't tryin' t'help him. I wanted him to feel bad because I did. I wanted that girl. I wanted him to pay for ignorin' me. But I was wrong. That's why I walked home in the rain.'

'I don't get it,' Right said.

Later that night Right slept on the foldout lawn chair that was Socrates' guest bed.

Socrates awoke to the snores of his friend. Ralphie and Linda, and Angel sitting at home with Warren, were on his mind.

The cold in his chest was breaking up and he was going to live.

'I ain't no niggah,' he said to himself.

He repeated that phrase.

'And if I ain't then you ain't neither,' he said to some imaginary friend. 'It's you and me, brother.'

Right sat up then. He stared across the small and disheveled room at his friend.

'You okay?' Right Burke asked.

'If you is,' Socrates answered.

The two old men laughed. Later they raised a toast, with apple brandy, to Lindas that they'd known.

EQUAL OPPORTUNITY

1

Bounty Supermarket was on Venice Boulevard, miles and miles from Socrates' home. He gaped at the glittering palace as he strode across the hot asphalt parking lot. The front wall was made from immense glass panes with steel framing to hold them in place. Through the big windows he could see long lines of customers with baskets full of food. He imagined apples and T-bone steaks, fat hams and the extra-large boxes of cereal that they only sold in supermarkets.

The checkers were all young women, some of them girls. Most were black. Black women, black girls – taking money and talking back and forth between themselves as they worked; running the packages of food over the computer eye that rang in the price and added it to the total without them having to think a thing.

In between the checkout counters black boys and brown ones loaded up bags for the customers.

Socrates walked up to the double glass doors and they slid open moaning some deep machine blues. He came into the cool air and cocked his ear to that peculiar music of supermarkets; steel carts wheeling around, crashing together, resounding with the thuds of heavy packages. Children squealing and yelling. The footsteps and occasional conversation blended together until they made a murmuring sound that lulled the ex-convict.

There was a definite religious feel to being in the great store. The lofty ceilings, the abundance, the wealth.

Dozens of tens and twenties, in between credit cards and bank cards, went back and forth over the counters. Very few customers used coupons. The cash seemed to be endless. How much money passed over those counters every day?

And what would they think if they knew that the man watching them had spent twenty-seven years doing hard time in prison? Socrates barked out a single-syllable laugh. They didn't have to worry about him. He wasn't a thief. Or, if he was, the only thing he ever took was life.

'Sir, can I help you?' Anton Crier asked.

Socrates knew the name because it was right there, on a big badge on his chest. ANTON CRIER ASST. MGR. He wore tan pants and a blue blazer with the supermarket insignia over the badge.

'I came for an application,' Socrates said. It was a line that he had spent a whole day thinking about; a week practicing. *I came for an application.* For a couple days he had practiced saying *job application*, but after a while he dropped the word *job* to make

73

his request sound more sure. But when he went to Stony Wile and told him that he planned to say 'I came for a application,' Stony said that you had to say *an application.*

'If you got a word that starts with *a, e, i, o,* or *u* then you got to say an instead of a,' Stony had said.

Anton Crier's brow knitted and he stalled a moment before asking, 'An application for what?'

'A job.' There, he'd said it. It was less than a minute and this short white man, just a boy really, had already made him beg.

'Oh,' said Anton Crier, nodding like a wise elder. 'Uh. How old are you, sir?'

'Ain't that against the law?' Like many other convicts Socrates was a student of the law.

'Huh?'

'Askin' me my age. That's against the law. You cain't discriminate against color or sex or religion or infirmity or against age. That's the law.'

'Uh, well, yes, of course it is. I know that. I'm not discriminating against you. It's just that we don't have any openings right now. Why don't you come in the fall when the kids are back at school?'

Anton leaned to the side, intending to leave Socrates standing there.

'Hold on,' Socrates said. He held up his hands, loosely as fists, in a nonchalant sort of boxing stance.

Anton looked, and waited.

'I came for an application,' Socrates repeated.

'But I told you . . .'

'I know what you said. But first you looked at my clothes and at my bald head. First yo' eyes said that this is some kinda old hobo and what do he want here when it ain't bottle redemption time.'

'I did not . . .'

'It don't matter,' Socrates said quickly. He knew better than to let a white man in uniform finish a sentence. 'You got to give me a application. That's the law too.'

'Wait here,' young Mr Crier said. He turned and strode away toward an elevated office that looked down along the line of cash registers.

Socrates watched him go. So did the checkers and bag boys. He was their boss and they knew when he was unhappy. They stole worried glances at Socrates.

Socrates stared back. He wondered if any of those young black women would stand up for him. Would they understand how far he'd come to get there?

He'd traveled more than fourteen miles from his little apartment down in Watts. They didn't have any supermarkets or jobs in his neighborhood. And all the stores along Crenshaw and Washington knew him as a bum who collected bottles and cans for a living.

They wouldn't hire him.

Socrates hadn't held a real job in over thirty-seven years. He'd been unemployed for twenty-five months before the party with Shep, Fogel, and Muriel.

They'd been out carousing. Three young people, blind drunk.

Back at Shep's, Muriel gave Socrates the eye. He danced with her until Shep broke it up. But then Shep fell asleep. When he awoke to find them rolling on the floor the fight broke out in earnest.

Socrates knocked Shep back to the floor and then he finished his business with Muriel even though she was worried about her man. But when she started to scream and she hit Socrates with that chair he hit her back.

It wasn't until the next morning, when he woke up, that he realized that his friends were dead.

Then he'd spent twenty-seven years in prison. Now, eight years free, fifty-eight years old, he was starting life over again.

Not one of those girls, nor Anton Crier, was alive when he started his journey. If they were lucky they wouldn't understand him.

2

There was a large electric clock above the office. The sweep hand reared back and then battered up against each second, counting every one like a drummer beating out time on a slave galley.

Socrates could see the young assistant manager through the window under the clock. He was saying something to an older white woman sitting there. The woman looked down at Socrates and then swiveled in her chair to a file cabinet. She took out a piece of paper and held it while lecturing Anton. He reached for the paper a couple of times but the woman kept it away from him and continued talking. Finally she said something and Crier nodded. He took the paper from her and left the office, coming down the external stairs at a fast clip. Walking past the checkers he managed not to look at Socrates before he was standing there in front of him.

'Here,' he said, handing the single-sheet application form to Socrates. Crier never stopped moving. As soon as Socrates had the form between his fingers the younger man was walking away.

Socrates touched the passing elbow and asked, 'You got a pencil?'

'What?'

'I need a pencil to fill out this form.'

'You, you, you can just send it in.'

'I didn't come all this way for a piece'a paper, man. I come to apply for a job.'

Anton Crier stormed over to one of the checkers, demanded her pencil, then rushed back to Socrates.

'Here,' he said.

Socrates answered, 'Thank you,' but the assistant manager was already on his way back to the elevated office.

★   ★   ★

77

Half an hour later Socrates was standing at the foot of the stairs leading up to Anton and his boss. He stood there waiting for one of them to come down. They could see him through the window.

They knew he was there.

So Socrates waited, holding the application in one hand and the borrowed pencil in the other.

After twenty minutes he was wondering if a brick could break the wall of windows at the front of the store.

After thirty minutes he decided that it might take a shotgun blast.

Thirty-nine minutes had gone by when the woman, who had bottled red hair, came down to meet him. Anton Crier shadowed her. Socrates saw the anger in the boy's face.

'Yes? Can I help you?' Halley Grimes asked. She had a jailhouse smile – insincere and crooked.

'I wanted to ask a couple of things about my application.'

'All the information is right there at the top of the sheet.'

'But I had some questions.'

'We're very busy, sir.' Ms Grimes broadened her smile to show that she had a heart, even for the aged and confused. 'What do you need to know?'

'It asks here if I got a car or a regular ride to work.'

'Yes,' beamed Ms. Grimes. 'What is it exactly that you don't understand?'

'I understand what it says but I just don't get what it means.'

The look of confusion came into Halley Grimes's face. Socrates welcomed a real emotion.

He answered her unasked question. 'What I mean is that I don't have a car or a ride but I can take a bus to work.'

The store manager took his application form and fingered the address.

'Where is this street?' she asked.

'Down Watts.'

'That's pretty far to go by bus, isn't it? There are stores closer than this one, you know.'

'But I could get here.' Socrates noticed that his head wanted to move as if to the rhythm of a song. Then he heard it: 'Baby Love,' by Diana Ross and the Supremes. It was being played softly over the loudspeaker. 'I could get here.'

'Well.' Ms. Grimes seemed to brighten. 'We'll send this in to the main office and, if it's clear with them, we'll put it in our files. When there's an opening we'll give you a call.'

'A what?'

'A call. We'll call you if you're qualified and if a job opens up.'

'Uh, well, we got to figure somethin' else than that out. You see, I don't have no phone.'

'Oh, well then.' Ms. Grimes held up her hands in a gesture of helplessness. 'I don't see that there's anything we can do. The main office demands a phone number. That's how they check on your address. They call.'

'How do they know that they got my address just 'cause'a some phone they call? Wouldn't it be better if they wrote me?'

'I'm very busy, sir. I've told you that we need a phone number to process this application.' Halley Grimes held out the form toward Socrates. 'Without that there really isn't anything I can do.'

Socrates kept his big hands down. He didn't want to take the application back – partly because he didn't want to break the pudgy white woman's fingers.

'Do me a favor and send it in,' he said.

'I told you . . .'

'Just send it in, okay? Send it in. I'll be back to find out what they said.'

'You don't . . .'

'Just send it in.' There was violence in this last request.

Halley Grimes pulled the application away from his face and said, 'All right. But it won't make any difference.'

3

Socrates had to transfer on three buses to get back to his apartment.

And he was especially tired that day. Talking to Crier and Grimes had worn him out.

He boiled potatoes and eggs in a saucepan on his single hot plate and then cut them together in the pot with two knives, adding mustard and sweet pickle relish. After the meal he had two shots of whiskey and one Camel cigarette.

He was asleep by nine o'clock.

His dream blared until dawn.

It was a realistic sort of dream; no magic, no impossible wish. It was just Socrates in a nine-foot cell with a flickering fluorescent light from the walkway keeping him from sleeping and reading, giving him a headache, hurting his eyes.

'Mr Bennett,' the sleeping Socrates called out from his broad sofa. He shouted so loudly that a mouse in the kitchen jumped up and out of the potato pan pinging his tail against the thin tin as he went.

Socrates heard the sound in his sleep. He turned but then slipped back into the flickering, painful dream.

'What you want?' the guard asked. He was big and black and meaner than anyone Socrates had ever known.

'I cain't read. I cain't sleep. That light been like that for three days now.'

'Put the pillow on your head,' the big guard said.

'I cain't breathe like that,' Socrates answered sensibly.

'Then don't,' Mr Bennett replied.

81

As the guard walked away, Socrates knew, for the first time really, why they kept him in that jail. He would have killed Bennett if he could have right then; put his fingers around that fat neck and squeezed until the veins swelled and cartilage popped and snapped. He was so mad that he balled his fists in his sleep twenty-five years after the fact.

He was a sleeping man wishing that he could sleep. And he was mad, killing mad. He couldn't rest because of the crackling, buzzing light, and the more it shone the angrier he became. And the angrier he got the more scared he was. Scared that he'd kill Bennett the first chance he got.

The anger built for days in that dream. The sound of grinding teeth could be heard throughout Socrates' two rooms.

Finally, when he couldn't stand it anymore, he took his rubber squeeze ball in his left hand and slipped his right hand through the bars. He passed the ball through to his right hand and gauged its weight in the basket of his fingers. He blinked back at the angry light, felt the weight of his hard rubber ball. The violent jerk started from his belly button, traveled up through his chest and shoulder, and down until his fingers tensed like steel. The ball flew in a straight line that shattered the light, broke it into blackness.

And in the jet night he heard Bennett say, 'That's the last light you get from the state of Indiana.'

★　　★　　★

Socrates woke up in the morning knowing that he had cried. He could feel the strain in the muscles of his throat. He got out of bed thinking about Anton Crier and Halley Grimes.

4

'You what?' asked Stony Wile. He'd run into Socrates getting off a bus on Central and offered to buy his friend a beer. They went to Moody's bar on 109th Street.

'I been down there ev'ry day for five days. An ev'ry day I go in there I ask'em if they got my okay from the head office yet.'

'An' what they say about that?'

'Well, the first day that boy, that Anton Crier, just said no. So I left. Next day he told me that I had to leave. But I said that I wanted to talk to his boss. She come down an' tell me that she done already said how I cain't work there if I don't have no phone.'

'Yeah,' asked Stony Wile. 'Then what'd you do?'

'I told'em that they should call downtown and get some kinda answer on me because I was gonna come back ev'ryday till I get some kinda answer.' There was a finality in Socrates' voice that opened Stony's eyes wide.

'You don't wanna do sumpin' dumb now, Socco,' he said.

'An' what would that be?'

'They could get you into all kindsa trouble, arrest you for trespassin' if you keep it up.'

'Maybe they could. Shit. Cops could come in here an' blow my head off too, but you think I should kiss they ass?'

'But that's different. You got to stand up for yo' pride, yo' manhood. But I don't see it wit' this supermarket thing.'

'Well.' Socrates said. 'On Thursday Ms Grimes told me that the office had faxed her to say I wasn't qualified for the position. She said that she had called the cops and said that I'd been down there harassin' them. She said that they said that if I ever come over there again that they would come arrest me. Arrest me! Just for tryin' t'get my rights.'

'That was the fourth day?' Stony asked to make sure that he was counting right.

'Uh-huh. That was day number four. I asked her could I see that fax paper but she said that she didn't have it, that she threw it out. You ever hear'a anything like that? White woman workin' for a white corporation throwin' out paperwork?'

Stony was once a shipbuilder but now worked on a fishing day boat out of San Pedro. He'd been in trouble before but never in jail. He'd never thought about the thousands of papers he'd signed over his life; never wondered where they went.

'Why wouldn't they throw them away?' Stony asked.

'Because they keep ev'ry scrap'a paper they got just as long as it make they case in court.'

Stony nodded. Maybe he understood.

'So I called Bounty's head office,' Socrates said. 'Over in Torrence.'

'You lyin'.'

'An' why not? I applied for that job, Stony. I should get my hearin' wit' them.'

'What'd they say?'

'That they ain't never heard'a me.'

'You lyin',' Stony said again.

'Grimes an' Crier the liars. An' you know I went down there today t'tell'em so. I was up in Anton's face when he told me that Ms Grimes was out. I told him that they lied and that I had the right to get me a job.'

'An' what he say?'

'He was scared. He thought I mighta hit'im. And I mighta too except Ms Grimes comes on down.'

'She was there?'

'Said that she was on a lunch break; said that she was gonna call the cops on me. Shit. I called her a liar right to her face. I said that she was a liar and that I had a right to be submitted to the main office.' Socrates jabbed his finger at Stony as if he were the one holding the job hostage. 'I told'er that I'd be back on Monday and that I expected some kinda fair treatment.'

'Well that sounds right,' Stony said. 'It ain't up to her who could apply an' who couldn't. She got to be fair.'

'Yeah,' Socrates answered. 'She said that the cops would be waitin' for me on Monday. Maybe Monday night you could come see me in jail.'

5

On Saturday Socrates took his canvas cart full of cans to the Boys Market on Adams. He waited three hours behind Calico, an older black woman who prowled the same streets he did, and two younger black men who worked as team.

Calico and DJ and Bernard were having a good time waiting. DJ was from Oakland and had come down to L.A. to stay with his grandmother when he was fifteen. She died a year later so he had to live on the streets since then. But DJ didn't complain. He talked about how good life was and how much he was able to collect on the streets.

'Man,' DJ said. 'I wish they would let me up there in Beverly Hills just one week. Gimme one week with a pickup an' I could live for a year offa the good trash they got up there. They th'ow out stuff that still work up there.'

'How the fuck you know, man?' Bernard said. 'When you ever been up Beverly Hills?'

'When I was doin' day work. I helped a dude build a cinderblock fence up on Hollandale. I saw what they th'owed out. I picked me up a portable TV right out the trash an' I swear that sucker get ev'ry channel.'

'I bet it don't get cable,' Bernard said.

'It would if I'da had a cable to hook it up wit'.'

They talked like that for three hours. Calico cooed and laughed with them, happy to be in the company of young men.

But Socrates was just mad.

Why the hell did he have to wait for hours? Who were they in that supermarket to make full-grown men and women wait like they were children?

At two o'clock he got up and walked away from his canvas wagon.

'Hey,' Bernard called. 'You want us t'watch yo' basket?'

'You could keep it,' Socrates said. 'I ain't never gonna use the goddam thing again.'

Calico let out a whoop at Socrates' back.

On Sunday Socrates sharpened his pocket knife on a graphite stone. He didn't keep a gun. If the cops caught him with a gun he would spend the rest of his life in jail. But there was no law against a knife blade three inches or less; and three inches was all a man who knew how to use a knife needed.

Socrates sharpened his knife but he didn't know why exactly. Grimes and Crier weren't going to harm him, at least not with violence. And if they called the cops a knife wouldn't be any use anyway. If the cops even thought that he had a knife they could shoot him and make a good claim for self-defense.

But Socrates still practiced whipping out the

knife and slashing with the blade sticking out of the back end of his fist.

'Hah!' he yelled.

6

He left the knife on the orange crate by his sofa bed the next morning before leaving for Bounty Supermarket. The RTD bus came right on time and he made his connections quickly, one after the other.

In forty-five minutes he was back on that parking lot. It was a big building, he thought, but not as big as the penitentiary had been.

A smart man would have turned around and tried some other store, Socrates knew that. It didn't take a hero to make a fool out of himself.

It was before nine-thirty and the air still had the hint of a morning chill. The sky was a pearl gray and the parking lot was almost empty.

Socrates counted seven breaths and then walked toward the door with no knife in his hand. He cursed himself softly under his breath because he had no woman at home to tell him that he was a fool.

Nobody met him at the door. There was only one checker on duty while the rest of the workers went up and down the aisles restocking and straightening the shelves.

With nowhere else to go, Socrates went toward

the elevated office. He was half the way there when he saw Halley Grimes coming down the stairs. Seeing him she turned and went, ran actually, back up to the office.

Socrates was sure that she meant to call the police. He wanted to run but couldn't. All he could do was take one step after the other; the way he'd done in his cell sometimes, sometimes the way he did at home.

Two men appeared at the high door when Socrates reached the stairs. Salt and pepper, white and black. The older one, a white man, wore a tan wash-and-wear suit with a cheap maroon tie. The Negro had on black jeans, a black jacket, and a white turtleneck shirt. He was very light-skinned but his nose and lips would always give him away.

The men came down to meet him. They were followed by Grimes and Crier.

'Mr Fortlow?' the white man inquired.

Socrates nodded and looked him in the eye.

'My name is Parker,' he continued. 'And this is Mr Weems.'

'Uh-huh,' Socrates answered.

The two men formed a wall behind which the manager and assistant manager slipped away.

'We work for Bounty,' Mr Weems said. 'Would you like to come upstairs for a moment?'

'What for?' Socrates wanted to know.

'We'd like to talk,' Parker answered.

★　　　★　　　★

89

The platform office was smaller than it looked from the outside. The two cluttered desks that sat back to back took up most of the space. Three sides were windows that gave a full panorama of the store. The back wall had a big blackboard on it with the chalked-in time schedules of everyone who worked there. Beneath the blackboard was a safe door.

'Have a seat, Mr Fortlow.' Parker gestured toward one of the two chairs. He sat in the other chair while Weems perched on a desk.

'Coffee?' asked Parker.

'What's this all about, man?' Socrates asked.

Smiling, Parker said, 'We want to know what your problem is with Ms Grimes. She called the head office on Friday and told us that she was calling the police because she was afraid of you.'

'I don't have no problem with Ms Grimes or Anton Crier or Bounty Supermarket. I need a job and I wanted to make a application. That's all.'

'But she told you that you had to have a phone number in order to complete your file,' said Weems.

'So? Just 'cause I don't have no phone then I cain't work? That don't make no sense at all. If I don't work I cain't afford no phone. If I don't have no phone then I cain't work. You might as well just put me in the ground.'

'It's not Bounty's problem that you don't have a phone.' Parker's face was placid but the threat was in his tone.

'All I want is to make a job application. All I

want is to work,' Socrates said. Really he wanted to fight. He wanted his knife at close quarters with those private cops. But instead he went on, 'I ain't threatened nobody. I ain't said I was gonna do a thing. All I did was to come back ev'ry day an' ask if they had my okay from you guys yet. That's all. On the job application they asked if I had a car or a ride to work – to see if I could get here. Well, I come in ev'ry day for a week at nine-thirty or before. I come in an' asked if I been cleared yet. I didn't do nuthin' wrong. An' if that woman is scared it must be 'cause she knows she ain't been right by me. But I didn't do nuthin'.'

There was no immediate answer to Socrates' complaint. The men looked at him but kept silent. There was the hum of machinery coming from somewhere but Socrates couldn't figure out where. He concentrated on keeping his hands on his knees, on keeping them open.

'But how do you expect to get a job when you come in every day and treat the people who will be your bosses like they're doing something wrong?' Weems seemed really to want to know.

'If I didn't come in they woulda th'owed out my application, prob'ly did anyway. I ain't no kid. I'm fifty-eight years old. I'm unemployed an' nowhere near benefits. If I don't find me some way t'get some money I'll starve. So, you see, I had to come. I couldn't let these people say that

91

I cain't even apply. If I did that then I might as well die.'

Parker sighed. Weems scratched the top of his head and then rubbed his nose.

'You can't work here,' Parker said at last. 'If we tried to push you off on Ms Grimes she'd go crazy. She really thought that you were going to come in here guns blazing.'

'So 'cause she thought that I was a killer then I cain't have no job?' Socrates knew the irony of his words but he also knew their truth. He didn't care about a job just then. He was happy to talk, happy to say what he felt. Because he knew that he was telling the truth and that those men believed him.

'What about Rodriguez?' Weems asked of no one in particular.

'Who's that?' Socrates asked.

'He's the manager of one of our stores up on Santa Monica,' Weems replied.

'I don't know,' Parker said.

'Yeah, sure, Connie Rodriguez.' Weems was getting to like the idea. 'He's always talking about giving guys a chance. We could give him a chance to back it up with Mr Fortlow here.'

Parker chewed on his lower lip until it reddened. Weems grinned. It seemed to Socrates that some kind of joke was being played on this Connie Rodriguez. Parker hesitated but he liked the idea.

Parker reached down under the desk and came

out with a briefcase. From this he brought out a sheet of paper; Socrates' application form.

'There's just one question,' Parker said.

7

'What he wanna know?' Stony Wile asked at Iula's grill. They were there with Right Burke, Markham Peal, and Howard Shakur. Iula gave Socrates a party when she heard that he got a job as a general food packager and food delivery person at Bounty Supermarket on Santa Monica Boulervard. She made the food and his friends brought the liquor.

'He wanted to know why I had left one of the boxes blank.'

'What box?'

'The one that asks if I'd ever been arrested for or convicted of a felony.'

'Damn. What you say?'

'That I musta overlooked it.'

'An' then you lied?'

'Damn straight. But he knew I was lyin'. He was a cop before he went to work for Bounty. Both of 'em was. He asked me that if they put through a check on me would it come up bad? An' I told him that he didn't need to put through no checks.'

'Mmm!' Stony hummed, shaking his head. 'That's always gonna be over your head, man. Always.'

Socrates laughed and grabbed his friend by the back of his neck.

He hugged Stony and then held him by the shoulders. 'I done had a lot worse hangin' over me, brother. At least I get a paycheck till they find out what I am.'

MARVANE STREET

1

Water seeped in under Socrates' boarded-up door to the street. The rain was hard and he had to put towels down at the cracks where the tiny streams tried to flow across his sleeping room. He listened to the rain pelting down on the tin roof and was happy that he didn't have to go to work that day. He picked up the throw rugs from the concrete floor and changed towels every hour or two. The couch he slept on was up on wooden blocks and the kitchen floor was elevated by worn linoleum tiles; there'd have to be a downpour to flood out the kitchen.

The rain seemed to get harder for a moment; the sound of water cascading over the drainpipe and crashing on the old barrel on the other side of his wall. Then it stopped. A gust maybe. But he hadn't heard the wind. Then the sound again. Not exactly water on the barrel. It was a little too hard.

The sound came back twice more before Socrates realized that it was knocking at his back door, the only working door.

He rarely had guests in good weather; never in the rain.

The boy was standing there, soaking wet.

'Hey, Darryl,' Socrates said. He moved aside so that the boy could come in.

'Hey.'

'What you doin' out in this rain?'

'I'ont know. Nuthin'.'

'You hungry?' Eleven-year-old boys, in Socrates' experience, were always hungry. Especially if they were black boys; especially if they were poor.

Socrates brought out a large bowl of chicken-and-rice gumbo from his new squat refrigerator. He heated the stew on the butane camping stove he'd gotten from an army surplus store downtown. Socrates bought everything from that store. His clothes and his shoes, his pocket knife and dishes. Ever since he started working for Bounty Super-market on Santa Monica, boxing and delivering groceries, Socrates had been shopping, buying necessities that were more like luxuries for the ex-con.

He cut raw onions into Darryl's bowl and then sprinkled ground sassafras and thyme leaves over it all. He put Darryl in the good folding chair and turned over the empty trash can for his own seat.

Darryl was shivering but didn't seem to know it. He ate the gumbo with a large spoon and didn't talk because his mouth was too busy working to fit in any words. Watching the boy's gluttony, Socrates had to stifle the rage that bloomed in his chest. He

96

wanted to slap the skinny boy out of his chair, to see him sprawled out on the floor. He wanted to pick Darryl up by those bony shoulders and slam him up against the wall.

He wished that some man had had that kind of love for him before he'd gone wrong.

He'd told Darryl that he could come over anytime he had a problem but this was the first time that the boy had returned. He was a troubled child with no father; one of those lost souls who did wrong but didn't know it – or hardly did.

'Thanks,' Darryl said after finishing his third bowlful. 'That was good.'

'How you doin', boy?' Socrates asked.

'M'okay.'

'How's yo' momma?'

'She fine. She got a boyfriend. Tyrell. He up in the house a lot. But she's fine. I guess.'

Socrates took Darryl's bowl to the sink and filled it with water. He tried to wipe off the ledge behind the basin but the plaster was crumbling and no amount of wiping could get it clean.

'You get dreams?' Darryl asked the broad-backed murderer.

'Sometimes.'

'What you dream about?'

'Whatever it is I want an' don't have. That's why they call'em dreams.'

'Oh, uh-huh.'

'What you dream about?'

'Nuthin'.'

Darryl sat in the plastic chair staring at the older man's chest. He seemed angry. Socrates was mad too. He could see that Darryl was in trouble. And trouble was always close to violence in Socrates' life. Even this, even his concern for the boy, bunched up in his biceps and played along his shark finlike knuckles.

'I got some pie up on the top shelf,' Socrates said.

'What kinda pie?'

'Do it matter?'

'I'ont eat no mincemeat pie. That shit is nasty.'

'It's peach. I got it at the sto'.'

'Yeah, I want some.'

Socrates brought down the pie. Only half of it was left. He cut it into two equal pieces and served it up on aluminum mess plates. When he ate the anger subsided a little. It was a good pie that they were going to throw away at Bounty. He took a bag of leftovers home at the end of every week from the store.

'You ever dream about somethin' you don't want?' Darryl asked.

'Well. Sometimes I don't think I want sumpin' when really I do.'

'But I mean somethin' that you really hate. Somethin' make you wake up scared and wanna run.' Darryl's eyes were looking back into the dream.

'You dreamin' 'bout that boy?' Socrates asked.

Darryl swallowed, but he didn't say a thing.

'What you dream?' Socrates put his hands in his pockets and leaned back on his trash can.

'We was in a big room, with all the lights out but you could still see. He was cut on his neck but he was walkin'. He didn't have no clothes on an' he was walkin' after me. He was screamin' an' I was runnin'. The room was really big but you couldn't see nuthin' 'cept for him . . .' Darryl shivered again.

Socrates wanted to hug the boy but he knew better. 'He catch you?'

'Naw, uh-uh. I always wake up 'fore he can. But he be there ev'ry night. I cain't hardly even take no nap but he there. I get ascared even to go in my bed.'

'What you think he gonna do if he catch you?'

'Pull me down an' make me dead like him. Burn the skin offa my bones like in that movie I saw.'

'Why he wanna do that, Darryl?'

''Cause I kilt'im. 'Cause he mad at me. 'Cause me an' Jamal an' them lef' him up there an' didn't even tell his momma that he dead. An' now he ain't even buried right. That's why.' Darryl started tapping his spoon against the metal plate.

'You wanna do somethin' 'bout that?' Socrates asked.

'Ain't nuthin' to do. Maybe I could take sumpin' make me sleep some.'

'That's why you come here? You think I got some sleepin' pills?'

99

'Naw. I could get them at school.' Darryl beat out a steady beat on his plate.

'Stop that bangin', little brother,' Socrates said. 'An' pay attention. As long as you alive you could do somethin'. That's what bein' alive is all about. When you dead then your doin' days is over. It's over for that boy. He's dead. He's dead an' you killed him an' now you feel bad. So you got to do sumpin'. An' since you did wrong now you got to do a good thing. Try an' balance it out.'

'An' then I could sleep?'

'I bet you could. Shoot. Why'ont you go on in the other room right now an' stretch out on my sofa. I'll make sure nobody come get you. An' then when you get up we'll talk about what you could do.'

Darryl had come over at about nine in the morning. He was asleep by ten. The rainclouds passed over at noon and Socrates went out in his small garden to turn the soil for the rose bushes he hoped to buy.

He was daydreaming about golden roses late in the day when Darryl came outside. His eyes were bleary but at least there wasn't a frown on his face.

'How'd you sleep?'

'Fine,' the boy said. 'How long was it?'

''Bout five hours. Maybe more.'

'Damn.'

'You go on home, Darryl. Come back tomorrow and we try'n figure out what you could do.' Socrates made a play of swinging his big fist at Darryl.

100

That was the first time he'd seen the boy smile.

'Bye,' Darryl said, and he waved to show that he meant it.

2

The next day was Sunday. Socrates didn't work on the weekends because the high school kids all wanted those hours.

Darryl came by but they didn't talk about what he could do to make up for murder. They had Kentucky Fried Chicken and Darryl took another nap.

Socrates gave Darryl the keys to his apartment and every day for a week he'd come home to find the boy sprawled out on his sleeping couch.

It wasn't until the following Saturday that Socrates had his lesson planned.

'You ever been down on Marvane Street?' Socrates asked Darryl after they'd finished a breakfast of pork sausage with scrambled eggs and green onions.

'Uh, well, Jamal been down there.'

'T'get his dick suck?'

'I'ont know. I guess.'

'You better tell yo' friend that he might lose his dick down there. Shit! I wouldn't wanna shake hands wit' none'a them crackheads.'

'Uh-huh.' Darryl picked up his spoon.

Before he could start his drumming Socrates said, 'We gonna go on down there today.'

'Where at?'

'Marvane Street.'

'What for?'

''Fore you could do sumpin' you gotta know what the problem is. The problem you got is down on Marvane,' Socrates said.

They walked, down the wide alley that went past Socrates' door, onto the main street and east – toward Marvane. The streets were full of people. Children and their mothers, older men propped up against abandoned storefronts or seated on some box or discarded chair. There were gangs of children, gangs of teenagers, gangs of young men and women; passing in cars blaring loud hip-hop music, walking down the street laughing and dancing, making jokes that sounded like threats.

'You in a gang, Darryl?' Socrates asked.

'Not yet.'

'You gonna be?'

'Maybe.'

'Maybe?'

'It ain't up t'me,' Darryl said. 'Sometimes you gotta get in wit' them – for p'otection. Right now ain't nobody fightin' on my street. But if they do then I gotta be wit' somebody. You cain't make it by yo'self in no war.'

'Hm!' Socrates wanted to say something but he didn't know what. Darryl knew a child's street better than he did. In those streets children died every day.

'That's yo' problem right there, Darryl.'

'What?' The boy looked around but he didn't see anything.

'To try'n think of a way that children don't get killed. Try'n make it better for whoever you can.'

It took about an hour to get to Marvane. It was a wide street with big houses that had been subdivided into apartments many years before. A few of the homes had burned down, leaving empty lots between the overpopulated buildings. The lots were full of garbage and refuse, temporary sleeping places, and small children at play.

At the back of one empty lot was a large single-story house. The windows had been boarded over and the only way in or out was a metal door. In the lot a dozen or so people stumbled around. Some of them were talking, some just listening to the music in their blood. Every now and then a solitary figure would come out of the fire door, or go in.

'That where Jamal go t'get his dick suck?' Socrates asked.

'I guess. I ain't never been.'

'Why not?'

'Sound nasty.' Darryl frowned and shook his head.

'That house is part of the problem,' Socrates said. He talked as they walked by, across the street.

'Yeah? What I'm s'posed t'do about that?'

'I don't know. All I do know is that it's part of it. Drugs killin' people faster'n heart attacks down here.'

'What's the other part?' Darryl asked.

They were already past the drug house and coming close to another place. There was a sign over the front door that read THE YOUNG AFRICANS. It was a rooming house that had been converted to offices. Young men and women, many in African-like clothing, could be seen through the windows and in the yard. There was a guard at the door. This man wore a black suit and a coal-gray T-shirt, sunglasses, and a short-brimmed hat.

'You been up there?' Socrates asked.

'Naw, man,' Darryl said, sounding like he was mimicking somebody he'd heard. 'Them niggahs don't make no sense.'

Suddenly Socrates broke out into laughter. There was a childish glee in his high-pitched wheezing. He slapped Darryl on the back, nearly knocking the boy down.

'You sure ain't no fool, Darryl.' Socrates laughed no more. 'No, you sure ain't.'

They kept moving. Three houses down, across the street from them and the Young Africans – on the same side of the street as the crack house – was a smaller dark house. There was a new chain-link fence around it. A fat man with a big black cigar between his lips was watering the lawn.

'Let's go up here, boy.' Socrates led the way up

104

to the high front porch of a rooming house directly across the street from the dark house. They went up to the top of the stairs and sat down.

'What we doin' here?' Darryl asked.

'What you see?' Socrates asked, motioning his head toward the house across the street.

'A house.'

'What else?'

'I'ont know. It's a house wit' a fat man waterin' wit' a hose.'

'What else?'

'I'ont know. Uh, it got, uh, let's see, um, it got three flo's. And, uh . . .' Darryl counted on his fingers while peering at the house. 'An' eleven windahs. It's dark. It got a new fence, an' uh, an' uh . . . That's it.'

'Uh-huh.' Socrates nodded. 'You want some Kool-Aid?' The ex-con pulled a flask out of the inside of his army jacket. He passed it over to his pupil.

The boy downed it all in one swallow.

'What now?' Darryl asked.

'Keep lookin'. Maybe you see a li'l sumpin' else.'

'Hey, Socco,' a voice said from inside the rooming house. Darryl and Socrates were watching the dark house. The fat man had gone inside.

'Hey, Right.' Socrates turned. With an aging man's groan he rose to shake hands with his friend.

Right Burke was old even to Socrates. A commando veteran of WWII, he had a withered left hand and he wasn't much taller, or sturdier, than Darryl. But his walnut eyes had all the strength a man could need. The first day Socrates saw those eyes he knew that they were the eyes of a friend you could trust.

'I'm here wit' my friend Darryl, watchin' our house.'

'Pleased t'meet'cha.' Right held out his hand to Darryl. The boy stood up and took the man's hand. Holding on, Right asked, 'You seen anything yet?' Then he winked and let go.

'Eleven windows,' Darryl said.

Right laughed and sat down with his guests.

'Where Luvia at?' Socrates asked.

'Down at church,' Right said. 'They makin' sweet potato pies for a street fair tomorrah. Shoot. You know if she was here she'da kick yo' ass offa these stairs by now.'

'Luvia run this house,' Socrates explained to Darryl. 'It's kinda like a private retirement home.'

'Uh-huh,' Darryl said, but his attention was on the house across the street. 'I don't see nuthin'. All I see is eleven windahs wit' the shades down.'

'Now you got sumpin',' Socrates said.

Darryl looked harder but the shades didn't seem like anything to him.

'It's a bright sunny day,' Socrates said.

'Yeah?'

'Then why they gonna have their shades down if it's so nice outside?'

'Uh, 'cause they sleep?'

Right laughed and said, 'That's a good one.'

'Ain't nobody in the yard,' Socrates said. 'Ain't nobody comin' over on a Saturday. Garage all closed up. You ain't seen it but there's a Ford van come in an' outta the garage late at night. An' you see that shade up on the third flo'? The one on the far right side.'

'Yeah,' said Darryl.

'Do it look different?'

'Kinda.'

'Kinda how?'

'Like it's shiny. I'ont know.'

'Yes you do too know. It is shiny. That's 'cause it ain't made'a cloth like the other shades. That one there is plastic. An' you know why?'

'Uhhh, uhhh, uhhh . . . 'cause they do sumpin' different in there?'

Both men laughed. Darryl frowned and looked down between his knees.

'We ain't makin' fun'a you, Darryl. Don't go poutin' on me now. It's just what you said is funny. You see, that there is a house fulla cops. They doin' what they call surveillance. Watchin'. Watchin' the Young Africans. An' you know why?'

Darryl was in too deep and he knew it. He hunched his shoulders and let his head loll to the side.

'They worried 'bout them young college Negroes. Maybe they makin' bombs down there. Even worse: maybe they gonna get all the other Negroes to vote. An' it's black cops too. Me an' Right

107

seen'em. Black cops spyin' on black college kids while Jamal right down the street gettin' his dick suck. Do that sound like the law to you, Darryl?'

The boy shook his head with a confused look in his eye.

'Three cops on ev'ry shift. Three shifts,' Right said. 'You know we figger that, with benefits an' expenses, they payin' at least twenty-five hunnert dollars a day just to look at them kids. Here you got twenty old people right here could hardly pay for food. It's a damn shame.'

'An' if that ain't bad enough there's a crack house runnin' almost next do',' Socrates said. 'Two houses down an' them cops been there . . . how long is it now, Burke?'

'Four weeks.'

'Four weeks,' Socrates continued. 'Four weeks. An' you know there's been half a dozen people shot or stabbed on this here block in the last four weeks. It takes the cops quarter of a hour at least to answer nine-one-one an' them cops in that house don't make a peep. Not a goddam peep.'

'Mm!' Right Burke grunted. 'Damn shame.'

'Socrates Fortlow!' a woman's voice declared. 'What the hell you doin' on my front steps?'

'Uh-oh,' Right said.

'Hey, Luvia,' Socrates greeted the gaunt-faced woman. She was coming up the stairs quickly. Socrates rose to meet her. 'This here is Darryl. Stand up, Darryl, an' meet Right's landlady.'

Darryl did what he was told. He stood up straight and put his hand out at the sapling-thin woman.

'Who's this, Socrates?' she asked.

'My friend. Ex-chicken thief. He's a boy lookin' for a good deed to commit.'

'Well let me tell you, boy,' she said. 'You wanna do somethin' good then you should get away from this man here. He anything but good.'

'That's okay, Luvia. You don't have to like me. But Darryl here might be comin' 'round sometimes. Just 'cause you hate all men I hope you still got a little heart for a man-child.'

Right Burke laughed and Luvia slapped his shoulder.

'Get offa my property, Socrates Fortlow! Git!' she yelled.

'See ya later, Right,' Socrates said. He and Darryl went down the stairs and back the way they had come.

3

'Why she hate you?' Darryl asked when they were down the block.

Socrates grinned and said, 'That's a good woman, boy. Good woman. She run that house for poor black folks when half the time she broke at the end of the month. If it wasn't for donations from her church you know the county marshal woulda repossessed by now.'

'But why do she hate you?' Darryl asked again.

''Cause she's a good woman.' There was a wistful note in Socrates' voice. 'And I'm anything but good. Luvia could smell the bad on me. All she had to do was to see me once an' she knew what I was. An' you know she's a Christian woman too.'

'But if she religious don't that mean she should forgive you?'

'Christians believe in redemption, that's true. But usually you have to die in order t'get it. I guess Luvia would say a few nice words if I died. But it would take somethin' like that. It sure would.'

They stopped for popsicles at a little store on Central and then went on toward Socrates' home.

'You have a good time, Darryl?' Socrates asked the boy. It was getting late in the afternoon. The sky toward the ocean was changing from dusty blue to a light coral color.

'Yeah,' the boy said tentatively. 'But I still don't know what I have to do. I cain't see nuthin' 'bout that crack house and the Africans. An' you know I ain't gonna get close to them cops. I'm just little. I need sumpin' little t'do.'

Socrates smiled. His legs were beginning to ache from the walk. 'What you think about them Young Africans? I mean, how come you don't like'em?'

'You know. They always talkin' like they know shit an' we stupid 'cause of our music or whatever, you know. I mean they up in their house tryin' t'tell

110

us how t'live an' they ain't no better. They ain't got no money or no nice car.'

'So? At least they're trying to make somethin' better. Right?'

'Maybe so. But I still don't have to like'em.'

'Let's stop a minute, little brother. My legs ain't young like yours is.' Socrates halted and leaned up against the wall of a boarded-over hardware store. He took a deep breath and smiled at the multicolored sky. 'I don't like 'em neither,' he said. 'I mean I like what they say but words ain't deeds. They don't know how to deal wit' people.'

'What you mean?' Darryl asked.

Socrates saw in the boy an honest question. He saw that Darryl really respected him, really wanted to know what he thought. The idea that Darryl wanted to hear what he had to say scared Socrates.

'You don't teach people, you love'em. You don't get a house and a printin' press and put up a fence. You do like Luvia. You open up your arms and your pocketbook. You don't have to worry 'bout no cops. Cops don't mean shit. But you don't let no crack house be on your street neither. Uh-uh.

'You got to love your brother. An' if you love'im then you wanna make sure he's safe.'

'That's like in a gang,' Darryl said.

'Yeah.' Socrates nodded. 'In a way it is. But in a way it ain't neither. The Young Africans like a gang. They got their code an' their colors. They ready to go to war. An' that's fine. Sometimes you

111

got to go to war. But most the times you should be helpin'. You should be laughin' an' eatin' good an' you should go to bed knowin' that they ain't nobody hungry on yo' street.'

Darryl was looking deeply into Socrates' eyes. He heard the word hungry. Socrates knew that he would.

'So it's only that lady hate you doin' right on Marvane,' Darryl said.

'Uh-huh. The only one gonna make black people feel good. The only one got a right to go to war.'

Darryl and Socrates started walking again. Neither one said anything until they reached Socrates' back door. They went inside and took turns going to the bathroom.

When they were sitting again Socrates asked, 'So what you gonna do now?'

'I gotta get home.'

'I mean what you gonna do, boy?'

Darryl stared at his mentor but there were no words in his mouth, no thoughts behind his eyes. Socrates was reminded of hours and years spent behind bars with nothing in his head. He remembered thinking that the only thing to life was feeling pain – or not feeling it.

'What should I do?' Darryl asked.

'I don't know, Darryl. Maybe, maybe you should dream.'

'Huh?'

'You still have bad dreams at night?'

'Not too much. If I do, an' I wake up, then I

think that I'm gonna do sumpin' an' I go back to sleep.'

'That's good,' Socrates said. ''Cause a boy needs sleep, you know. How he gonna go to school and answer hard questions like the ones you got if he don't get his rest?'

'What questions?'

'Marvane Street.'

Darryl cocked his round head to the side and nodded. He blinked and then nodded again.

Socrates put his hand on Darryl's shoulder. 'You know there's only two things that a poor boy like you gotta do, Darryl.'

'What's that?' Darryl put his hands up and touched Socrates' arm. It was a light touch, and brief.

It didn't hurt at all.

'First you got to survive,' Socrates said. 'Then you got to think; think and dream.'

Darryl nodded. He said, 'But I prob'ly get killed.'

'No you won't, boy. I won't allow that.'

'But how could you stop it?'

'I don't know,' Socrates said. 'But I ain't alone. If they start shootin' on your block, then you come here to me. If I cain't help ya we go to Right and Luvia. She got a whole church wit' her.

'You see, Darryl, a boy like you might have to go underground.'

'Like in a hole?'

'Not a real hole. But you might have to hide

113

from people. You be there but they won't know it.'

'But what if they wanna get me at school?'

'Then you get outta school an' learn someplace else.'

'I could do that?'

'You can do anything, boy. Just as long as you alive – you could do anything.'

4

That night Socrates had a dream:

He dreamt that he was sleeping in a tiny room, no larger than a closet. He was dreaming about the rain when there came a violent knock on the door. He jumped up and crouched down at the end of his canvas cot, scared of the powerful blows that had awakened him.

'Socrates!' a bass voice boomed. 'Socrates!'

And then Socrates woke up.

But when he went back to sleep that big voice called out his name again. This time it was even louder and Socrates lurched awake.

Five times the voice called to him and five times he woke up panting. He decided on that last awakening that he wouldn't run from the voice again.

He fell asleep and the voice called.

'What you want?' Socrates yelled, ashamed of himself for shivering.

'Come on out here!' the voice commanded.

Socrates opened the door. He found himself standing before a towering, jet-black man. A man with a broad broad nose and sensual big lips. The man's eyes were stern and his shoulders were wide as a sail.

'Come on!' the big man said. And they were walking outside in the driving rain.

The weather was strange to Socrates because even though it was night and cloudy and raining, in the far-off distance he could see the moon illuminating a small hill. The light from the moon lit the field through which he and his big companion traveled.

They walked for a long time, until Socrates' legs began to ache. They came at last to a giant stone arch that had the words SOULS END chiseled into its crown. Beyond the arch, bathed in rain and lit by a golden moon, stretched a graveyard that went on for hundreds of miles. The graveyard went so far that at its farthest limit it reached into daylight.

It was the graveyard for all the black people that had died from grief. Each grave was marked by a small granite stone, hardly larger than a silver dollar.

'Here!' the big man said. He handed Socrates a spade. 'We got to dig all'a them up now. It's time.'

'All that!' Socrates yelled over the squall.

'Every one,' the big man said.

'I cain't do it!'

'But you could try!'

'It'd kill me!'

The giant gestured toward the graves with a hand even larger than Socrates'. 'We all die!'

Socrates came awake again. He sat up and laughed so hard that he had to get up out of the bed. He laughed so hard that his side hurt and he sank to his knees. After laughing he ran to the toilet and threw up the beef and mushroom gravy he'd had for dinner the night before.

'It was like . . .' he said to Right Burke a few weeks later. 'It was like I was a child seein' lightnin' for the first time. The light show made me all giddy but the thunder scared me down to my boots.'

MAN GONE

1

It was five thirty-six p.m. by Socrates' new digital watch when Corina Shakur came calling. He knew it was her knocking but he went to the door anyway. She stood a few feet back, showing no intention of coming any closer.

'Have you seen'im?' the tall young woman asked, her lips and nose curling into disgust.

'Hi, Corina,' Socrates answered, smiling. 'What you doin' here? You lookin' for Howard?'

Corina was too angry to answer his polite question. She moved her head from one side to the other and clutched her shoulders, clenching them tightly as if trying to make her body into a fist.

'Come in,' he said. 'Come on in.'

Before she could decline, Socrates turned around and went back into his small apartment. He took the two and a half steps across his kitchen and went through the doorless doorway into his sleeping room.

'I'll get you a chair from in here, Corrie,' he

called over his shoulder. 'I fount me some old kitchen chairs an' patched'em up.'

Socrates picked up the yellow vinyl-and-chrome chairs and carried them back to the kitchen. Corina was standing in the doorway, the sun silhouetting her long curving figure.

'Come on in, Corrie,' Socrates said. He was squinting and smiling and feeling spry.

'I ain't got time to be wastin' 'round here, Socrates Fortlow.' Corina held back, speaking to him as if she were calling across a river.

'Okay,' Socrates said. He positioned a chair to face her, then sat himself down. 'But you don't mind if I take a load off, now do ya?'

'Do what you want.'

'You lookin' for Howard?' Socrates asked.

'You seen'im?'

'Why'ont you come on in, Corina?' he asked in mild frustration.' 'Don't you want some coffee? You know I don't get that many young lady guests. It be nice for me just t'see you sittin' in my chair.'

Corina sighed and then said, 'I cain't stay long. The kids is wit' my sister.'

Socrates jumped up and turned sideways to hide the glee he felt when Corina came in. He moved the chairs to his folding card table and then struck a match to light the butane stove that sat on the sink.

'Where's Howard?' Socrates asked as he ran tap water into a saucepan.

'You ain't seen'im? Really?' Corina asked. There were no tears but her voice was small, making her sound like a sad girl.

'No.' Socrates put the pan on the stove. He sat down in a plastic chair that had once been his only seat. 'What happened?'

Socrates had always liked Corina. She had the kind of face that showed her feelings no matter how hard she tried to look mad. She carried her shoulders high and her body was long and straight except for a small belly that looked comfortable and down-home.

Corina never trusted Socrates but he didn't hold that against her; he knew any woman who didn't trust him probably had good sense.

'We had a fight last night an' he left.' Corina sat back in the chair and turned her head to avoid crying. 'He ain't never stayed out all night.'

'Hm!' Socrates got up to check his water even though he knew it wasn't boiling yet. 'What you fight about?'

'It wasn't nuthin'. I just said that maybe he could get a job down wit' McDonald's or sumpin' like that while he was waitin' t'see if he could do computer operations. You know he ain't had a job for nine months an' they cut back my hours at Penney's. All I said was that he could do it in the meantime, while we was waitin'.'

'An' he didn't like that? What's wrong? Don't he wanna work?' Socrates took a yard of cheesecloth and folded it over on itself twice, then he took a

119

can of MJB coffee and scooped three tablespoons of the grounds into the center of the cloth square.

'No,' Corina protested. 'He ain't lazy. He just proud. He say he too smart to be burnin' burgers fo'kids.'

'He ain't too proud t'let his wife go out an' make all the money, now is he?' Socrates brought together the corners of the cheese-cloth to form a little sack that he fastened by tying a string midway at the neck.

'Howard ain't afraid to work,' Corina said. 'He had a good job wit' the city parks, but you know they had all those layoffs.'

Socrates stood there, coffee ball in one hand and tin funnel in the other. 'But that was almost a year ago. You know Winnie an' li'l Howard ain't gonna stop growin' just 'cause their daddy cain't buy'em clothes.'

'That's right,' Corina declared. 'I tried t'tell'im that it don't matter what somebody might think. All that matter is what his kids feel.'

Socrates put the coffee cloth in the top of the funnel and wedged the tin spout in the mouth of an hourglass-shaped Pyrex jug.

'He ain't called or nuthin'?' Socrates sat back down.

'No.'

'Then he's a fool,' Socrates said. 'Man got a woman like you to get out on these dangerous streets an' go to work ev'ry day. Woman have his kids an' feed'em too. Uh. You know I be workin'

120

at McDonald's in the afternoon and Burger King at night.'

Socrates showed Corina his best grin. A trace of a smile skimmed her pouting lips.

'I ain't askin' fo'too much,' she complained. 'You know I go to work at JCPenney's, do all the housework, and then I got to be wit' them kids ev'ry second they ain't in the house. I let'em out just once by theyselves an' the bullets'll start flyin'.'

'I know it,' Socrates said. It was the truth but he was saying something else to the wife of his friend. 'You got to have eyes in the back'a your head to live in this world, girl. Eyes in the back'a your head, ears cocked, an' two fingers to the wind.'

Corina had a large space between her two front teeth. That smile was like a diamond to the miner Socrates.

'You want me to go out an' help you look for Howard?' the excon asked. He was staring hard at Corina.

'I'ont know, Mr Fortlow. Maybe Howard get mad if he knew I was tellin' his business around.'

'So what if he get mad? Shoot! He lucky he don't come home an' find some other man up in his bed.'

'No.' Corina shook her head vigorously and stared right into the older man's eyes. 'It ain't nuthin' like that goin' on.'

'I know, Corrie. You a good woman. Lovin' yo' kids an' yo' man, you ain't got no time to be actin' a fool. But I was just sayin' that Howard cain't leave no beautiful woman all alone an' expect the dogs t'stay down. Woman like you need somebody wit' all the hard work an' love you put out. That's why I just cain't understand it.'

'Understand what?' Corina asked. The look on her face opened a vein in Socrates' heart that he thought had died along with Muriel – the woman he'd murdered decades before.

For a moment Socrates couldn't speak. The blood flowing made him afraid that his heart was going bad. The chair underneath him seemed to shift.

'Uh, well,' he mumbled. 'I cain't see leavin' a woman you love for even one night. You wouldn't never want that woman to think that you could leave her. 'Cause she's your life. Your life.'

Corina Shakur wore simple jeans and a buff chamois shirt. Her hair was tied back with a polka-dotted blue-and-white handkerchief. Her sockless feet were in red sneakers. She clasped her hands and leaned forward. Not one bit of fear showed in her gentle face.

'You lose somebody, Mr Fortlow?' she asked.

The question hung there between them for five seconds, ten.

'Water's boilin',' he answered softly.

Socrates poured the steaming water from the saucepan into the funnel. Slowly dollops of the dark brown liquid dripped into the Pyrex jug. Socrates watched the jug closely as if that was part of the job of making coffee.

'Did you?' she asked.

Socrates swallowed hard. He poured a little more water and the flow increased. He took two thick mugs from the shelf and placed one down on the table near Corina.

'Sorry we cain't go in the other room,' he said. 'But I sleep in there too. It's a mess.'

'I don't mind sitting here,' she said.

Her eyes followed him as he brought the coffee over and poured.

'You take anything?' he asked.

'Sugar,' she said.

He had cubes in a bowl on the shelf. He held it as Corina fished out three lumps. He spent longer than necessary finding her a spoon.

She stirred while looking at him.

'You lose somebody, Socrates?' she asked again.

Socrates sat down and cleared his throat. He sipped his black coffee and coughed once more. 'I had a girl love me like the mornin' – once.'

'Back east? Howard said that you come from back east.'

'Indiana,' Socrates said.

'She leave you?'

Socrates turned his head to regard Corina Shakur. She was twenty-three years old; thirty-five years younger than him. But she knew things that he could only guess at. She had birthed children. She probably believed in God. She woke up in the morning thinking about how things could get better, or stay good.

123

'What was her name?' Corina asked.

'You want Howard back, Corrie?'

'I guess.' She looked down at her long fingers. 'I get kinda fed up is all. You know I try an' make things good for him, but he's so mad all the time. I try'n tell'im that he got to get over that. An' he know it but it's like it's too much for him.' Corina shook her head and sipped the sweet coffee. When she ran the tips of her fingers around the rim of the mug Socrates felt his heart clatter again. 'He wanna go dancin' an' to clubs like when we was goin' out, but we got kids now. What can I do about that? My sister cain't be takin' them all the time. I mean, I cain't help it if he too proud. I cain't work two jobs 'cause he won't work one. But if I say it then he get mad. I just don't know if it's worth it.'

Corina gazed at the floor but her eyes held the knowledge that Socrates was watching her. He watched until Corina was almost finished with her coffee.

'Could I say sumpin' to you, girl?' If Socrates had had a hat he would have held it over his heart.

'What?'

'I mean, I don't want you to get mad or to think that I'm tryin' to do sumpin' behind Howard's back. I couldn't do that.'

'Okay, Mr Fortlow. What you have to say?'

'You want some cake? I got some day-old devil's food from Bounty up in the closet.'

'No. I don't want no cake. I wanna hear what you got to say an' then I have to go.'

Socrates put his strong hands on his knees and leaned forward. 'You're a beautiful woman, Corina. Smart and sure and the kinda woman a man could count on. What they used to call a good woman back home. An' when I look at you I find a part'a me hopin' that that fool don't come back. 'Cause you know I wanna be in your door wit' flowers an' baby toys. You know I just sit here an' look at you an' I can see all the things in my life that I missed.'

Corina glanced over her shoulder at the door.

'Don't worry, honey,' Socrates said. 'I don't know what you heard about me but I'm not tryin' t'do nuthin'. And this ain't no secret sidetrack kinda thing neither. I would tell Howard what I'm tellin' you. I'd tell'im this very minute. 'Cause I don't have nuthin' t'lose an' I know it.

'Black men always be talkin' 'bout how hard life is on'em, but most of 'em don't e'en know the half of it. They too proud, huh. Ain't no pride like chirren; ain't no pride like a woman lovin' her man.' Socrates felt the sheen of sweat across his face; he heard the sexual fever in his own voice.

Tears sprouted in Corina's eyes and she didn't try to hide them.

'Right after you leave I'm gonna go find Howard and I'ma tell him what I just said to you. An' if he don't listen I'ma come up to your door wit' a job and candy for the kids.' Socrates stood up and Corina followed suit, like a small sail caught in a larger boat's wake.

125

He led her to the door and whispered, 'Don't worry. The kinda luck I got he prob'ly be home 'fore you are.'

Corina listed forward and then stopped, then she swayed forward again and kept going until her full lips were at the corner of Socrates' mouth. The kiss was a testament that she had heard his words; she wasn't afraid of how he felt.

2

He watched her go through the tiny garden and into the alley that ran past his gate. She half turned to catch a glimpse of him as she went.

A sideways look and half a kiss, Socrates thought. *Maybe if I wait another twenty years I might get a hug too.*

He went back into his kitchen feeling exhausted, the way he did on weekdays after taking the bus home from work. He sat down, took a deep breath, and then said, 'You could come on out, Howard.'

Howard Shakur came out of Socrates' sleeping room. The look on his fat face would have scared most men, but Socrates didn't care.

'You gonna fight me, boy?' the ex-con asked simply. ''Cause if you are I hope you got some in-surance for them babies.'

'What the hell you mean by lettin' her in here an' talkin' to her like you did?'

126

'You want some whiskey, Howard?' Socrates gestured a tired hand toward the cabinet under his sink. 'There's some whiskey down under there.'

Howard squatted down and came out with a fifth of PM whiskey. He stood up making a fat man's grunt and took two glasses from the shelf.

'What the hell you mean by tellin' Corina all that shit?' Howard said as he settled into the chair his wife had been sitting in.

'I ain't said nuthin' t'her that I didn't say to you a hour ago. I told you you was a fool.' Socrates took a short swig of the cheap whiskey and grimaced.

'But it was the way you was talkin', man. You tryin' t'get over on my woman?'

'You damn right I was. What you think, Howard? A woman look like she do an' she gonna go out an' bust a gut workin' full-time. That stuff is just like gold.'

'That's my wife you talkin' 'bout, man,' Howard Shakur said. He downed his glass and poured another.

'No it ain't.' Socrates shook his head and put his glass down. 'Uh-uh.'

'What you mean she ain't mines? Whose wife is she if she ain't mines?'

With speed that Socrates rarely showed he snapped forward and caught Howard by the wrist.

'Ow!' Howard shouted. He tried to pull away but the older man's grip was too strong for him.

'Let me tell you sumpin', boy. Long as you out here, away from that girl, she belong to whoever she

127

want. Ain't no man gonna say, 'Naw, I better stay 'way 'cause Howard might decide to come back one day.' Fuck that! Woman like Corrie make a man boil.' Socrates pushed Howard back so hard that he flew over backwards in his chair.

Howard jumped to his feet, ready to fight. Socrates rose to meet him. His blood was hot. He wanted to do something strong. If it wasn't with that girl at least he could break Howard's jaw.

But Howard hadn't had quite enough whiskey to be a fool. He snorted but that was the most of it.

'I thought you was my friend,' Howard said.

'You ain't got no friends when it come to a woman like Corrie, Howard. That's what I was tryin' t'tell you 'fore she got here. That's a woman you got there, man. She ain't no dog. She ain't no car for you to park somewhere and walk off on. She's a woman an' she needs her a man. Now she prefer that man to be you; at least right now. But you know I will be over there day after tomorrah. I will. Then you could be free and I could be happy.'

'That ain't right, brother.' Howard shook his head. 'Ain't right at all. I come here an' tell you my problem an' then you gonna run out after my old lady.'

'You said you don't want her. Ain't that what you said?'

'I said that I couldn't live up there no more. She always doggin' me.' Howard set his chair up and sat back down. He poured more whiskey and glowered at the tabletop.

'You see,' Socrates said. He held his hand against his chest. 'I don't mind that kinda doggin'. I don't mind a woman tellin' me when I'm wrong. She wanna kick my ass an' then kiss my lip . . . shit, you know I be the first one on line.'

'But she's my wife,' Howard said.

'Then get yo' ass home an' act like it.'

'You cain't tell me what to do,' Howard growled. 'I go home when I want to.'

'If you still got a home t'go to.'

They drank the bottle clear. Howard had more whiskey but Socrates felt its effect too. He muttered, 'If you cain't show a fool the door then you gots t'show'im the floor.'

'What you say?' Howard asked angrily.

'Fuck you,' Socrates said.

'I'ma get on outta here,' Howard said, but he made no move to lift his bulk from the chair.

'Howard,' Socrates said. 'You ever think about Corina fuckin' some other brother?'

The younger man glowered but stayed quiet.

'You know,' Socrates continued. 'Some little dude. Him gruntin' an' twistin' 'round like some goddam snake. An' here's you wife just singin' out his name an' smilin' like she's seein' Jesus.'

Howard opened his mouth – to get more breath.

'You know that ain't too bad.' Socrates held the empty bottle upside down over his glass. After a moment he realized that there were no more drops coming. 'Naw, not too bad. 'Cause you gonna find

129

you some other girl to sing for you. An' you gonna believe that that new girl got a better song. But you might not be thinkin' 'bout what happen after that skinny boy get up offa Corina. He gonna go get one'a your old undershirts an' wipe hisself off, an' then he gonna go in the other room and yo' kids, Winnie an' li'l Howard, gonna jump up sayin', "Daddy! Daddy!"'

Socrates sat back. When his hand left the table the bottle fell and shattered on the floor. Both men looked at the broken glass.

'But you got it better'n me, Howard. You got it better'n me. 'Cause even if you a fool at least you got a woman who had your babies. Even if you a fool an' never see them kids again – at least you had'em.'

Howard fell forward out of his chair. He went down on one knee and then stood up grunting.

Socrates heard him go but didn't see him leave. His eyes were wandering across that tabletop, looking at the walnut finish of the paper glued to the cardboard sheet.

3

Socrates Fortlow, a convicted murderer who was released (on his birth-day) after twenty-seven years in prison, washed up using the water out of his kitchen sink. He splashed on cologne from a sample bottle that he'd bought off a man selling odds and ends from a blanket on the street. He wore black jeans and a drab green turtleneck shirt. In the pockets of his army jacket he had five Hershey bars with almonds and a Mexican-made sterling silver ring inlaid with blue stones. He'd bought the ring from the man who'd sold him the cologne.

Socrates walked eleven long blocks to Howard and Corina Shakur's little stucco house on 121st Street. He hadn't heard from either one of them in a few days. But that was no surprise. Socrates didn't have a phone, Howard was probably still mad at him, and Corina had a family to take care of.

There was a plastic tricycle lying on the tiny porch. The screen was shut but the door beyond it was open. Socrates felt his heart pumping. He waited a second and then knocked on the aluminum frame.

'Momma!' Winnie shouted from somewhere inside. 'The do'!'

Corina looked good in her orange housedress. When she saw Socrates a smile filled her soft features. She opened her mouth to say something. Socrates hoped that it would be an invitation but instead she called out, 'Howard. Howard, Socrates is here.'

She unlatched the screen and ushered him in. He sat down on a spindly sofa couch that had thin pine legs. Winnie was playing with a doll on the floor and little Howard was digging a finger in his nose and gaping at the powerful newcomer.

Howard came out of the kitchen and Socrates rose to meet him.

'Hey,' Howard said and they shook hands.

'Hey, how you doin'?' Socrates replied. 'I just come by to see how you folks is.'

'We're fine now, Mr Fortlow,' Corina said. She was beaming at Socrates.

'Yeah,' Howard said. 'Got me a job at Pronto Pizza.'

'Really?'

'Yeah. They just lost an assistant manager an' wit' my experience wit' the city they hired me on probation. Only pay six twenty-five a hour right now, but it could go up to eight eighty-five in six months if I work out.' All the time he spoke, Howard watched Socrates distrustfully.

'Sit'own,' Corina said. Howard took the chair facing the couch and Corina ran into the kitchen to bring out a kitchen chair. She was smiling and happy.

'What shift they got you on?' Socrates asked as he settled back down.

'Three to eleven. But I could get days if I get seniority. I could be a manager if it works out.'

'That's really good, Howard.' Socrates meant the words but he could only whisper them.

'When Howard come home I told him what you said, Mr Fortlow.' Corina smiled. 'I told him I could get a man to work two jobs for me.' She reached out to hold Howard's hand.

'Yeah,' Socrates said. 'Howard ain't no fool. No sir. Winnie?'

'Yeah?' the little girl answered. She was sitting in the corner talking to her black baby doll.

'You want some chocolate?'

The girl whirled around and looked at her mother. Corina nodded and the girl did too. When Socrates took the Hershey bar from his jacket, little Howard started whining and holding his hands up over his head.

'Caddy! Caddy!' the baby cried.

'Share wit' your brother now,' Howard said.

''Kay, Daddy.'

They visited for a while and then Socrates rose. Corina told him that they were going to have a dinner the following Sunday with their parents and that he should come too.

'You like my father, Socco,' Howard said, smiling for the first time. 'He old, like you.'

As he walked away from the door he heard, 'Bye, Mr Fortlow!' and turned to see Winnie, with Corina standing over her, at the screen.

4

On the way home Socrates saw a round dinette table, with three broken legs, lying in the street. It was made from maple wood and deeply scarred. Socrates hefted the table on his back, using the leather strap from his pants to hold it around the one good leg. He put the other legs under his arm and carried the heavy table for nine blocks. He made a deal with himself that he could keep the table if he could walk the whole distance without putting it down.

His deal included the special circumstance that he would accept help if it was offered. But nobody offered. No one even seemed to notice Socrates and his labor.

The last three blocks had his lungs hurting and his knee joints were on fire. He almost dropped the whole thing when he reached the wooden gate of his garden. But he held on with the grip of his baby finger of the left hand. He made it through to the back door and then let go.

Socrates came to dinner the following Sunday. The elder Mr Shakur was as fat as Howard. They had a good time together and when Socrates left he told Corina that he'd invite them over to dinner sometime soon.

For the next three weeks Socrates worked on the table. He used carpenter's glue and metal ties to restructure the broken and splintered legs. He cut grooves in all four legs and the tabletop, then glued them together using a bag full of sand to hold it all down. He sanded the wood and then puttied the gashes. He restained the table and brushed on polyurethane to seal and protect his work.

Every night after coming home from his job boxing groceries at Bounty Supermarket. Socrates worked the wood. He'd go to bed rubbing his fingertips together, feeling the hot blisters of hard work.

When he was finished he walked over to the Shakur residence and invited the whole family over to dinner.

He prepared greens and rice, and beef tripe cooked with tomato sauce, garlic, and vodka. The tripe was a recipe that he got from the butcher at Bounty.

He served the meal on his rebuilt maple table.

He had pies and ice cream for the children; Seagram's and soda water for their parents.

Howard wasn't mad at Socrates anymore. He had his wife and job, he had his kids. The food was good and Corina drank more than she was used to. She talked silly baby talk with the children and made eyes at both of the men.

Socrates stood up straight from the table and said, 'Corina, I have something for you.'

'Oh?' she said, holding her head at a slant. 'And what is that?'

'This here table that I found and put back together again,' Socrates said. 'I wanna give it to you-all.'

'No,' Corina said. Maybe she even sobered a little. 'That's too much. It's so nice.'

'Yeah,' Howard said.

'Yeah,' echoed Socrates. 'I fount it an' put it back together. An' all the time I was thinkin' 'bout you two. 'Bout how I wanted to say how, how wonderful yo' wife is, Howard. An' how anytime you wanna walk out or give up you could look at the hard work I put in this table.' Socrates was talking to Howard but his eyes were locked with Corina's. ''Cause you know I'm out here waitin' an' you cain't slip up a damn bit.'

Little Howard made a wild scream just then and laughed. Corina turned her own amazed smile on her son and picked him up. He slapped her on the nose and laughed again but she ignored it.

'You feel up to it, Howard?' Socrates asked his friend.

'Up to what?'

'We gotta carry it over your house. Turn it upside down an' it should be easy.'

'You really wanna give us this?' Howard asked. He was squinting at his friend.

'Just think's me when you sit down to dinner, man. Tha's all. Think'a me out here an' you in there – safe an' warm wit' yo' family.'

THE WANDERER

1

When Socrates Fortlow was released from prison he ran just as if he had gone over the wall. There was no family that wanted to take him in. There were no old friends except for other men who had been released from prison and now lived in the shadows of Indianapolis, Gary, and Chicago.

They paid Socrates twelve hundred thirty-two dollars and sixty-three cents for his twenty-seven years behind bars. He put the money in his pocket and took a bus to Los Angeles.

He had three reasons to go there.

The first was that even though he had been born and half raised on a farm he no longer knew the country. He couldn't live the slow rural life and so he needed a city.

His second reason for escaping west was that the prison he'd come from was drafty and cold. The only cold he wanted from that day on was chill in the one thousand dollars' worth of beers that he planned to imbibe.

He learned in prison that L.A. was a big rambling bunch of towns and that everybody was in too much of a hurry to remember faces, places, times, and events. An ex-con would need that kind of anonymity.

And so he got on a Greyhound hunched over, sullen, and silent like some kind of fugitive. He ran as far as California and then he burrowed in, hating every policeman, every clerk's glance, and every footstep behind him.

He ran because he knew that in Indiana the cops would know him. If they knew him they'd try to bring him in every now and then. And if anyone tried to put him in a cell again he would try his best to kill them.

Socrates Fortlow was running for his life.

Within a week of his release from prison, eight years ago, Socrates had his first fight. He was confronted, in the alley that passed his door, by a bulky young man named Charles Rinnett. Charles, trying to impress his grinning friends, had claimed that Socrates was an 'old Dumpster-divin', rag-pickin', homeless mothahfuckah.'

Socrates was only fifty at that time and even though he was more than twice the age of Charles he convinced the young man by argument, and a strong hand, that he wasn't homeless and that he had never eaten from the garbage.

'Sometimes a broke nose is all you young boys understand,' Socrates said while standing over the heckler. He'd knocked Charles to the ground three times before the youth got the idea to stay down. The young men around them stopped laughing at Socrates and started making fun of their friend.

Charles never spoke to Socrates after that day. He grew older and more somber and could be seen, now and then, collecting bottles and cans on the streets of Watts. Socrates watched Charles for all those years as he turned meaner and shabbier.

If he could have, Socrates would have told Charles that he was sorry for breaking his nose; that he was just recently out of the penitentiary when they had their fight. In the penitentiary you had to hurt somebody in your first few days on the block because you had to show that you weren't a punk. A fight was no more than a housewarming in the joint.

Sometimes, as the years passed, Socrates would have imaginary talks with Charles. He'd ask the yellow-eyed sloucher why he stayed around those same old streets.

'Why you out here actin' like a hoodlum child when you a man should be makin' sumpin' out yourself?' Socrates mouthed the words silently on the bus coming home from his new job at Bounty Supermarket.

'An' what you doin' so special, old man?' the Charles in Socrates' mind responded. 'You live in that rat hole an' take the bus to yo' sto' ev'ry day. What you makin'? What you doin'?'

139

'I got a job, man,' Socrates whispered. 'I get up an' go to work. I get a paycheck. I got me a bank account.'

The lady sitting in front of Socrates got up. At first he thought that she was getting off, but then she just changed seats.

He put his fingers to his lips and concentrated on keeping quiet. But then his mental friend said, 'You a niggah just like me, Socrates Fortlow. Your shit stink an' you down on the bottom of the white man's ladder – right next to me. I cain't go nowhere an' you cain't neither.'

'I can too!' Socrates said loudly. 'I go wherever I damn please!'

No one turned around to see what Socrates was talking about but they heard him – they could have testified to his vow.

2

The very next Saturday morning, Socrates got on a bus headed for Santa Monica. The big blue bus was empty except for him and the driver – a black woman who liked to talk.

'Yeah, all my kids down Atlanta,' the driver said. 'You know colored people always on the move. Always tryin' to get somewhere fast. I done told'em they might as well stay here. I told'em that what you got to do is to make a stand somewheres. But they don't listen. They say that they ain't nobody givin' no chance for no colored up here. Shoot. I ain't askin' nobody to give me a damn thing. Nobody give you nuthin', now do they, mister?'

'Well,' Socrates said. 'They might give you one thing.'

'Oh,' said the driver. 'What's that?'

'A good kick in the pants.'

That got the driver laughing. She laughed so hard that Socrates was afraid she'd run the red light they were approaching. But she didn't. The brake trumpeted like a bull elephant and the bus swayed to a halt, giving Socrates the feeling that he was riding inside of a great wave.

'What you doin' out here today?' the driver asked. 'You work out here?'

'I come out here 'cause I wanted to,' Socrates answered. 'You don't have to spend yo' whole life livin' in a cave like some goddam caveman. I wanna see the ocean. I been in L.A. for eight and a half years an' I ain't seen the ocean once.'

'Hm! Well at least you know it,' the driver said, sneering with the satisfaction of the truth. 'That's what's wrong wit' so many people. Here they got the world right out there in front'a them an' they complainin' that they ain't nuthin' they could do. I'm wit' you. Pay your fare an' see what's what.'

Socrates got off the bus at Lincoln and Pico. He wandered around that neighborhood until he happened upon the big blue ocean.

There was a ribbon of sidewalk running down

the beach, about a hundred yards from the water. Near-naked men and women with good bodies traveled up and down the pedestrian road by walking and running, by blade skates and bicycle. There were skateboarders and surfers and men and women in wet suits. Everybody seemed hard at work at their recreation.

Socrates was reminded of the prison yard.

He had the same feeling he'd get when he was let out of solitary confinement. The yard was a wonderful place after a few weeks in the icebox. There was sunlight and the company of men. There were weights and checkers and magazines and talk. He was still in jail but he had the feeling of freedom after being let out of the punishment box. Even jail could feel good if they let you stretch your legs and squint at the sun once in a while. The sun was hard and strong on the beach that day. Socrates took off his shoes and socks and put them in the pockets of his army jacket. Then he took off the jacket and slung it over his shoulder.

There were hardly any people down near the water. A few joggers; just as many dogs.

At the shoreline the surf was loud. It boomed and hissed and sang in a chorus of drowning bells. The sound was everything down near the water. The whole world was the blue god's song.

'God ain't nowhere near here, child,' Socrates' aunt, Bellandra Beaufort, used to say. 'He's a million miles away; out in the middle'a the ocean somewhere. An' he ain't white like they say he is neither.'

'God's black?' little Socrates asked the tall, skinny woman. He was sitting in her lap, leaning against her bony breast.

'Naw, baby,' she said sadly. 'He ain't black. If he was there wouldn't be all this mess down here wit' us. Naw. God's blue.'

'Blue?'

'Uh-huh. Blue like the ocean. Blue. Sad and cold and far away like the sky is far and blue. You got to go a long long way to get to God. And even if you get there he might not say a thing. Not a damn thing.'

Socrates walked for miles on the curving beaches. The surface of the sand was hot from the sun but cool when his foot sank to the layer of moisture below. He went north past Malibu and on toward the blue of the water and sky. He stayed close to the ocean remembering his aunt's sermons about how God was always beyond reach but how people were always trying to get there.

Men ain't never satisfied wit' what is an' that's why they's only one out of a hunnert that's happy.

He ate three bananas and a peanut butter and jam sandwich from his pockets. The soft sand, the wind, and the wild seas made him feel as if he were staggering under some angry god's rage.

The sun rose high and was hot on his head. But a cold wind tore off the waters and chilled his bones.

Socrates knew that Charles Rinnett had never been this far – not on his own, not sober, not with his eyes open.

'Out of the icebox,' he said to himself. 'And into the sea.'

3

Socrates walked on, freezing and burning and feeling a freedom that he only ever dreamt about when he was a child on his bitter aunt's lap. The sun arched high above, almost washing out the blue in the sky, and then began to descend.

Socrates saw seashells and syringes half buried in the surf;

he saw a group of gulls rending the corpse of a brown dog; he saw the patterns of high tide rippled in the dry sand. Here and there was salted foam, like dried semen, sketched into sandy depressions.

Everything was harsh and beautiful the way he'd always known life to be. Socrates felt every breath and wondered if he could leave the life he'd made back down around Charles and his grinning fool friends.

If he got tired he sat down. There was fruit and sandwiches enough in his pockets. He knew that he should turn around but he had the notion that there might be something waiting for him up ahead. Something that he could take home. Something that would keep him from forgetting what he had seen and felt.

He passed many people on the way north but never spoke. Sometimes he'd nod and smile; now and then his greeting was returned.

Toward the later afternoon he saw a couple walking his way from far up the shore. A man in layers of gray and a woman dressed in bright clothes. He was large and she was slight with a youthful gait. She swung one hand back and forth while the other arm was wrapped around her lover's waist.

They were certainly lovers, Socrates could tell that. He was older and she was the kind of child that drove older men crazy. There was a double passion in them. His gait was heavy, deliberate; hers so lighthearted that she was almost in flight there next to him.

Socrates hoped that they would keep walking in his direction. He wanted to see their faces and smile at them.

From afar Socrates thought the man might have been black, or Mexican, or maybe he was just a very tan white man. The girl had to be white though. Her skin almost shone in the afternoon sun.

It didn't matter. Nothing did in the breathlike wind of the blue ocean; the screaming and chiming and hissing of some language that was older than men were, older than life itself. Socrates heard the words of that blue god in the base of his brain.

It made him feel crazy and struck him dumb.

Slowly the couple came toward him.

He trudged on.

When they were less than a hundred feet distant, Socrates was sure the man was black but he was no longer positive about the girl. Her skin was olive closer up.

The girl or woman, white or black, whatever she was, waved at Socrates and his heart jumped. He felt like a child again about to meet new friends at the playground sandbox.

4

'Hey, man,' said the large Negro, who was dressed all in gray. 'What's happenin'?'

He took Socrates' hand in a powerful grip. It was rare that Socrates encountered a man as strong as he was. He might have been aging, he might have lost his wind, but Socrates could still lift a forty-gallon trash can brimming with water and walk it a full city block.

'Hey,' the young woman said with one quick breath. Her skin was amber and her long hair was everything from blond to brown; from straight to curly. Her eyes might have been green. But it was her face that gave Socrates pause. The features were sparse on a long, horselike skull.

The extended bone of her nose came down, broadening a little toward the generous lips. Her cheeks were high but the sloping curve of her forehead diminished their effect.

She was a beautiful woman-child, not more than seventeen, and strange to look at – almost not human.

'We were watchin' you,' the girl said. 'Gordo thought that you were a soldier like him but I said no. I said that you weren't ever in any army. You walk like nobody ever taught you how to march.'

Socrates smiled and nodded.

'Well?' the man asked.

'Well what?'

'Were you in the army?'

'Not hardly,' Socrates said.

The girl socked Gordo in the upper arm and shouted, 'Hah! I win!'

'You want a drink?' Gordo asked Socrates. He slung a large gray backpack from his shoulders and sank to his knees in the sand. 'This is Delia.'

Delia stuck out her hand and when Socrates took it she pulled so that he would sit down with them.

'What's your name?' she asked.

'Socrates.'

'Wow. Far out,' she mouthed. Maybe she was whispering but Socrates couldn't hear her over the sound of the waves.

Gordo pulled a quart bottle of cheap red wine from the backpack.

'We got weed too. You want some smoke?' he asked.

'Wine'd be fine.'

Gordo had a boy's face with hair that had gone more than half gray; salt-and-pepper through his mustache and eyebrows. He unscrewed the bottle top and took a deep swig of the red wine.

Socrates took the next drink.

Delia held the bottle to her open mouth and poured the wine in, spilling some down her multicolored patchwork vest. She laughed and handed the bottle back to her man. Gordo twisted the bottle into the sand.

'What brings you out here?' Gordo asked Socrates.

'Nothin' that I could tell,' Socrates answered. 'Just out for a walk. I do that about every twenty years or so.'

Gordo smiled. 'You want somethin' to eat? We got chili and tortilla chips.'

'And soda,' Delia added.

'Sure,' Socrates said. He was thinking that he should go home, back to Watts. He was thinking that he was too far out. A voice in his head actually said, 'Go home now, Socrates,' but the wind and the water made the voice small and insignificant.

Delia pulled up her leather skirt and folded her bare legs in the sand.

'There's a bunch of driftwood a mile or so back there. Up toward the canyon,' Gordo said. 'We could go on up there. Nobody'll see a fire.'

Socrates was staring at those long brown legs.

When Delia looked into his eyes her grin turned into a silent laugh.

5

They went back up the beach about a mile, then under Pacific Coast Highway through a concrete drainage ditch. The steep canyon they entered was narrow and nameless. It went about a thousand yards into the Santa Monica Mountains and then came to a halt. Throughout the dry streambed were tangled piles of driftwood, brought in on countless high tides.

'You come out here much?' Delia asked Socrates as they picked their way through the creek bed.

'Never been up here before.'

'It's funny 'cause it's kinda wild and then it's like civilized too.' She pointed up toward the edges of the steep canyon walls. At first all Socrates saw was the sky. The blue was darkening toward night. Then he saw the lights; electric lights from houses that perched at the top of the canyon. Houses that seemed to be teetering; on the verge of tumbling down the cliffs. Some of them had already fallen prey to mud slides and erosion. One such disaster had brought a full wall of salmon-pink cinder blocks crashing down to the creek bottom.

'If I could have me a house,' Gordo said, looking

149

up at the canyon walls, 'that's where I'd have mines.'

'Why's that?' Socrates asked.

''Cause the ground up there just wearin' away, right out from under them.' Gordo grinned in the fading sunlight.

'But . . .' Socrates said, thinking again that he should be on his way. 'But that don't make sense.'

'Ground under you an' me, an' even Delia there, is wearin' out. Ground is hungry to be your grave, man. Ev'rybody walkin' 'round an' talkin' like the ground is up solid under them . . .' Gordo snapped his fingers loudly. 'You could be gone just like that. Just like one'a them houses up there.'

Delia moved close to Gordo's side. She picked a dry leaf from his hair.

'Ain't no use in hurryin' the process,' Socrates said.

'But,' Gordo said, 'at least up there you know for a fact that it's gonna happen. At least up there you know you got to live.'

Gordo took three of the blocks and laid them flat, their long sides facing in toward each other in a kind of ritualistic circle. Delia piled as much driftwood as she could between the cinder bricks.

From his pack Gordo pulled out a beaten-up tin pot that held three cans of Hormel chili. He also took out a large bag of tortilla chips and an eight-pack of cherry-flavored Coca-Cola in cans.

'It's my birthday,' Gordo said. 'This is my party.'

'You always come out here for your birthday?' Socrates asked.

Gordo looked him straight in the eye, his aging boy's face grim with concentration.

'No,' he said at last. 'Never been here for my birthday before. But I always go someplace special. And this here is the most special one.'

'Why's that?'

Gordo reached into his bag and came out with a long slender candle. It was tapered and deep red. Gordo held the candle up and smiled. 'My birthday candle,' he said.

Delia was busy opening the cans of chili with a pocket can opener that was no larger than a quarter. She dumped the fat-clotted dark brown contents of each can into the pot.

Gordo brought the quart of wine to his lips and finished it in one long draft. Then he took the candle and screwed it into the bottle's neck.

'For everyone born somebody dies,' Gordo intoned. 'For every birthday we celebrate the dead.'

He lit the candle as solemnly as a priest. He was on his knees in front of the flame, his arms hanging helplessly at his sides.

Delia wedged the pot in between the cinder blocks and set the wood on fire with a cigarette lighter. The flames glared brightly and at the same time the sun sank behind the drainage embankment.

It was as if she had called up night with a gesture.

151

Delia, lit by the fire, seemed to be surrounded by darkness while the rest of the canyon was in the early onset of twilight.

Socrates felt the chill of evening. He sat down to put on his socks and shoes.

'Where you from, girl?' he asked to break the spell of Gordo's silent reverie.

'Ohio.'

'What about your parents?'

She shrugged and smiled, pulled her skirt way up on her thighs, and went down on her knees.

'I killed twenty-six people,' Gordo said. It might have been the only thing that could have dragged Socrates' eyes away from those legs.

'How many?'

'Twenty-six. The last one was twenty-six years ago. Skinny little slant-eyed mothahfuckah wasn't no bigger than a hunnert an' thirty pounds. Here I played football at L.A. High School an' he nearly kilt me. Nearly did. Nearly did.' Gordo gazed off toward the fire.

'Vietnam?'

'This here is the last candle,' Gordo said. 'The last one.'

He took a twig from the ground and lit it on the flaming wick of his blood-colored candle. The crooked stick winked and flickered on the evening breeze, like a butterfly of flame.

'I always come out with a girl and drink and celebrate one of the men I done in. I light'em candles one by one and eat and drink a toast.'

'What you want me for?' Socrates asked.

'We just saw you, man. That's all. You know, it's kinda like you pick up what you find on the beach. That's life on the beach.'

'Uh-huh,' Socrates said.

'You want some?' Delia asked. She'd piled a tin plate with tortilla chips and used an empty can to scoop chili over it.

Socrates took the plate along with a tiny white plastic fork. 'Thank you.'

She made another plate for Gordo, who took it gravely, with both hands.

'You eatin'?' Socrates asked the girl.

'I don't eat meat,' she said and then produced an orange from the inside of her cloak. She bit into the peel, spat out the rind, and then began to squeeze and suck at the hole she'd made.

Socrates tried to control his breath as he watched her cheeks and teeth and tongue working at the fruit.

'You got a car?' Gordo asked.

Socrates felt prickles across his bald scalp. 'You sure you ain't killed nobody in twenty-six years?' he asked.

Gordo's white smile flashed on his dusky face. He let out a low chortle.

Socrates felt his weight against the soft, giving ground. If he rose up quickly his feet would sink in the sand. The image of a painting that he'd seen in the prison library came into his mind. It was in a book called The History of

153

European Art. He didn't remember the painter's name.

It was a dark scene. Two men, sunk in the ground up to their knees, were hitting each other with cudgels. They were bloody and tired but they were stuck in the ground and had to keep on fighting forever. They were big men too. Bigger than the mountains that lay behind them.

'That's it, brother,' Gordo said. 'Nineteen sixty-nine, November third. It wasn't far out from the camp. He jumped at me with a stick knife but I heard him . . .' Gordo's eyes glistened in the firelight.

Evening had come.

'Where you comin' from, brother?' Gordo asked.

'Prison mostly.'

'What you in for?'

'Murder.'

'You killed a man?' Delia asked.

Socrates didn't answer her.

'How long you in prison?' Gordo asked.

'Twenty-seven years.'

'For killin' one man?' Gordo was really surprised.

'It was a man and a woman. I raped her too,' Socrates said, wondering at the spell of the ocean. 'And then there was three convicts I killed but nobody ever knew it, at least nobody could ever prove it. And then there was all the men I brutalized and molested, robbed and threatened. I either committed a crime or had a crime done to me

154

every day I was in jail. Once you go to prison you belong there.'

'You kill anybody hand-to-hand?' Gordo asked. His body was tense, his head still like a predator's.

'I did it all wit' my hands. All of 'em. I ain't never used no weapon. I had 'em but I ain't never used one.'

6

Gordo nodded and relaxed a bit.

'I went from high school to heroin by way of Vietnam,' Gordo said. Delia had her head in his lap, she was looking up into Socrates' eyes. 'Everything was stronger there. The drugs, the rain, the sun, and the enemy. You could put him in the ground but he'd just pop up again. Pop right back up at ya. After a while all you felt was tired. Tired.'

The exhaustion of war descended on Gordo. His shoulders slumped and the plate tilted in his lap. He couldn't speak or even lift his spoon. The man seemed so tired that Socrates wondered how long he would be able to draw breath.

Then Delia talked about orphanges and shopping malls and how she was nobody and how much she liked that because there wasn't anybody she wanted to be.

'You wanna come over there and fuck, Socrates?' Delia whispered when Gordo started to nod.

155

Socrates looked at Gordo first. He was ready to fight but Gordo hadn't even heard.

'What you say?' Socrates asked.

'You heard me. It's okay. You like me and it's a special day. We could go right over there.'

Delia held out a hand and Socrates took it. She pulled at him but there no strength in the girl. She leaned over and kissed his hand, biting it lightly. Socrates glanced at Gordo; now he was staring up at the stars thinking that there were stronger stars in Vietnam – no doubt.

Delia bit Socrates' lip and pushed her tongue along the line of his teeth. She pulled at his hands again, and he stood up. They walked to the edge of the light and embraced. Delia let her weight go as if she wanted to fall to the soft sand. But Socrates stayed upright, looking at Gordo staring at the stars.

Delia kissed him again and there was the magic of passion, but that passion was in the wind and the moonlight; that passion was perched dangerously at the sides of the canyon. It wasn't sex that he wanted. All that he needed he already had.

Delia felt it too. She let her arms fall but still leaned against him.

'I'm gonna go,' Socrates said.

'Oh.' Delia sounded honestly disappointed. 'Stay. We don't have to do anything. Come on.'

Socrates waved at Gordo and said, 'See ya.'

The vet waved back. 'See ya.'

On her tiptoes Delia gave Socrates a girl's kiss

156

on the lips. It was wet and soft and tasted of ocean salts and orange peel.

7

Socrates staggered back down the way he'd come; down near the water where the sand was firm and wet. The waves followed him, crashing against the shore and breaking into foam that was almost phosphorescent in the moon's stark light. It was, Socrates felt, the ocean's laughter.

And it was funny. He thought of Delia writhing in the sand with Gordo, her hemplike hair sporting small flames from the cookfire. He thought of Charles Rinnet, grown old before his time, pushing his stolen grocery cart down Hooper and Central and Florence.

He walked a long way and then stopped. His legs felt as if someone had laid a live wire against them. It was all he could do not to fall down. He strode up to where the underbrush and cliffs met the sand. There he found two large cardboard boxes. Abandoned. He fit the boxes together behind a thorny bush. Once inside he tried to keep the thought of coffins out of his mind.

The wind played against the paper walls all night; the hollow sound of rushing air and the slither of gathering sands. The wind was so strong the boxes would have blown away save for Socrates' weight. The wind pressed the side of the box

157

against him. He leaned into the pressure dreaming of his Aunt Bellandra's lap. In the morning he saw half-erased paw prints in the sand around his shelter. It made him happy to think of some dog guarding his frail home.

The sun glared down so strong that the sea seemed tame. When he raised his arms, bellowing as he stretched, hundreds of seagulls cried and broke into flight. He could see where they'd been resting in a flooded clearing just past his thorny corner.

He wondered about Delia and Gordo but did not return to their grotto. Instead he wandered back toward the blue buses and home.

Somewhere along the way Charles Rinnett's voice came to him.

'You think that shit mean sumpin'?' the phantom sneered.

'That talk is over,' Socrates whispered as he imagined Charles Rinnett blowing away on a breeze.

LESSONS

1

'What she say?' Darryl asked with little interest. He and his only friend, Socrates Fortlow, were sitting on a redwood bench in Carver Park in Watts.

'She didn't say nuthin'.' Socrates was remembering his mother and how he was so surprised that she had gotten older even in his dream. Her hair, the little he could see of it under her Sunday hat, had gone white and there was a heaviness to her face.

'That's why I thought she was real,' he said out loud.

'Say what?' Darryl looked around nervously at the ragged trees.

'I mean,' said the ex-convict, 'when she died, when I was in jail, she was only fifty-two. But she was way older than that in the dream. It was like she never died and just grew older and older.'

'Huh,' the boy said. In the few months since he'd left home to come live with Socrates he'd shot up four inches but hadn't gained a pound. He was long and bony, almost as tall as the hefty, hard-muscled Socrates.

'Ain't you listenin' t'me, boy?' Socrates glanced in the direction that Darryl kept looking. 'You see'im?'

'Not yet,' Darryl said. 'But he always comin' from over that way.'

'Well stop lookin' over there. He gonna know how scared you are he see you lookin'. Here, look at me.'

Darryl turned his head and squinted at Socrates. He was trembling.

'So what you think?' Socrates asked the boy.

'What I think about what?' Darryl whined.

'About my dream, that's what.'

''Bout yo' momma?'

'Yeah.'

'Was she nice to you?' The boy's adolescent voice cracked from approaching manhood and fear.

'Oh yeah,' Socrates said. 'My mother was the only one stuck by me. The only one.'

''Cause you know,' Darryl said, 'I be dreamin' 'bout Yvette Frank sometimes.'

'Yeah?'

'Uh-huh.' Darryl nodded like a much younger boy. 'She be naked an' tell me how much she like me.'

'An' then you wake up wit' yo' dick all hard?'

Darryl leaned down quickly, plucking a long blade of tattered grass from underneath the bench.

160

He twirled the shoot, squashing it until the light-colored pads of his forefinger and thumb took on a greenish tint.

'That's okay,' Socrates said. 'That's how you dream when you a boy. You dreamin' 'bout manhood.'

Socrates stared out across the littered lawn of the park. At a picnic bench not far from them four men had begun a lively game of dominoes.

'Twenty-fi'e!' Trevor Brown shouted as he slapped down his bone.

Socrates recognized Trevor from the South Central Flea Market and Fair down at the Avalon Shopping Center. The mall had gone bust in 1988. Now the supermarket and stores were broken up into stalls that people rented by the day, the week, or the month. You could get anything from music discs to power tools at the Flea Market Fair.

Trevor Brown sold T-shirts that his daughter hand-painted with images of African warriors and statuesque women.

Socrates had rented a stall now and then to sell junk that he'd collected and repaired in his spare time. That was before he'd become a food packager and delivery man for Bounty Supermarket.

When Trevor raised his head in a victorious grin he caught sight of Socrates.

Socrates waved and Trevor gave him a happy nod.

Beyond the men came a group of three boys – twelve to fourteen years old. Tough-looking children with tennis shoes that had no laces and jeans that hung low on their hips. They seemed heavy in their big coats, ambling forward like a mob of unruly bear cubs.

The men stopped their game a moment to gauge the threat of the children.

Darryl looked up from his mangled blade of grass. He put his hand on Socrates' thigh.

'That him?' Socrates asked in a voice that held absolutely no emotion.

'Uh-huh.'

'Then let's get wit' it.'

'I ca . . . I ca . . . I cain't.'

'You got to, Darryl. They ain't no other choice.'

Darryl's eyes pleaded with Socrates but the ex-con showed no sympathy. He stood up and walked away. He went in a wide arc so as to avoid the attention of the rolling gang of boys.

He went over to the group of men playing dominoes.

'Hey, Trevor,' Socrates hailed.

At that same moment the head bear cub, Philip, yelled, 'Hey, punk. I told you to stay outta here.'

2

'Your boy's in trouble over there, Mr Fortlow,' Trevor said when Socrates made it to their table.

He hadn't looked back until then. He didn't want to witness Darryl running scared. But Darryl wasn't running. He faced the shorter, heavier Philip. The other two boys stayed a couple of yards back. Darryl was holding out his hands in a reasoning posture.

Good, Socrates thought, with those long arms he got the advantage.

'You hear me, Socco?' Trevor Brown asked.

'Say what?' Socrates was watching the boys closely.

The men around him were talking, asking questions, but Socrates just stared. Nothing was real except those boys.

Philip took a wild overhand swing at Darryl, who leaned back, wobbled a little bit, and then bounced forward with a textbook right cross. The fist found its target on Philip's chin.

The hard little gangbanger didn't even flinch.

Darryl had good training, and more courage than most, but he didn't have enough muscle to back it up.

Socrates took a deep breath and held it. Someone put a hand on his shoulder. Socrates stiff-armed whoever it was that touched him. He heard the man's *Wholp!* and the sound of the dominoes skittering around.

Darryl produced a steak knife from somewhere in his pants but Philip slapped it right out of the boy's bony hands.

Somebody shouted, 'Hey, what the . . .' but Socrates didn't hear the rest of what was said because he was moving. Philip's fist made a meaty connection with Darryl's jaw, and even though the lanky boy was tying up his attacker the way Socrates had taught him to, it wouldn't be long before Darryl was hurt bad.

Socrates kicked off his shoes to get better traction in the grass. Close to sixty, he didn't feel old because hot blood was moving in him. He went quickly and quietly behind Philip's two friends.

Darryl doubled over from a fist in his gut.

The first boy went down from a slap behind his head.

Darryl screamed and twisted on the ground as a heavy foot barely missed his face.

'Hey . . .' was all the second boy could get out before he was slapped senseless by Socrates.

But Philip hadn't seen his friends go down. He hit Darryl with a flying body slam that ended in a laugh and a hippy sexual grind.

Darryl was screeching while Socrates disarmed the prone boys. He pulled a Glock, a rusty .22, and a switchblade from their clothes.

'Turn over!' Philip shouted.

Darryl was lying on his stomach with his hands and arms up over his ears.

'Turn over, pussy boy!' Philip's words were loud and slurred with passion. With his left hand he was trying to force Darryl to turn over. In his right hand he held up a .45 automatic.

'Help!' Darryl shouted, and then, 'Pleasepleaseplease.'

Socrates slapped the gun from the upheld hand.

164

When Philip turned around to see who it was, he got slapped so hard that he tumbled over twice, coming to rest in a heap.

'All right!' shouted a domino player. The others were cheering.

The other two boys were trying to rise but they didn't know where they were.

Socrates yanked Philip up by his arm. The boy was out. Socrates pinched his cheek hard and twisted. The pain woke him up.

'You see me, boy? You hear me?'

Philip's head moved, maybe it was a nod.

'Who you?' he asked.

Socrates released him so that Philip stood under his own power, on uncertain feet. Socrates was going to hit him one more time; once more and he'd think twice before he messed around with Darryl again. Socrates grinned, thinking, *Three times, an' he'd be dead.*

But before even one more blow Trevor Brown shouted out, 'Watch it! Watch out, Socco!'

The big man swung around, ready for his death – or someone else's. But what he saw almost made him laugh.

Darryl stalked toward them on stiff legs, Philip's .45 automatic held out before him in both hands. The boy lurched from side to side as he approached, the pistol pointing anywhere and everywhere.

When he came up beside Socrates, Darryl stopped and brought the wavering muzzle up to about two feet from Philip's chest. Philip's widely spaced small eyes came awake while he was staring at that gun.

Darryl looked to Socrates and then back at Philip. Darryl's mouth opened in a wide, silent yowl. His eyes darted back and forth between friend and foe.

'Don't look at me,' Socrates said.

Darryl's aim got straighter and Philip took off. He ran straight past Darryl, then crouched low to avoid Socrates' wide grab. He ran screaming toward the domino table as Darryl swung around to fire.

'Shit!' a domino man shouted.

They all went down to the ground but it wasn't necessary. When Socrates touched Darryl's arm the boy released the gun, letting it fall unfired to the grass.

3

'I was scared,' Darryl sulked, staring down at Socrates' pitted linoleum floor.

'That was a damn good punch you give that boy,' Socrates answered. 'Right on the chin.'

Darryl sat up a little straighter.

They'd come home carrying the knife and three pistols in a brown paper bag.

'You stood up for yourself, Darryl,' Socrates said. 'That's all a black man could do. You always outnumbered, you always out-gunned.'

'But they gonna still be after me,' Darryl said. 'They still gonna wanna get me.'

'That's right,' Socrates agreed, nodding. 'But now you done stood up. Now you done your best, so you don't have nuthin' t'be sorry for – not ever again in your life.'

'How that gonna help me?'

'You done your job, Darryl. Now leave it up to me.' They had smoked ham hocks, served with mustard, and rice for dinner.

'What's wrong, boy?' Socrates asked.

'I'ont know. Nuthin' I guess. I mean if I was like you I wouldn't have no problems.'

'Hm. If you was like me you woulda spent ten years on a dirt farm hopin' your daddy got drunk enough to pass out 'cause if he didn't you'd get your ass whipped with thick cord.'

'He did that to you?' Darryl asked. 'For nuthin'?'

'When he fin'ly died my momma cried, not 'cause he was dead but because we lost the farm. But I was happy until I realized without him I didn't eat ev'ry night. No, Darryl, you don't wanna be like me.

'You don't wanna run wild in the street treatin' women like they was dogs. Fightin' an' stealin' an' actin' up till they put you in jail. Naw, man, you wanna get out from under all that shit. You got to.'

'But I'ont know how,' Darryl said.

After the dinner Socrates said, 'You take my bed tonight. I'll sleep out here on the couch. You worked hard today, you need a good sleep.'

* * *

167

As he fell off to sleep, Socrates knew that Darryl couldn't stay with him any longer. One day that gang of boys would find him. They'd either kill him or make him one of their own.

Maybe not. It didn't always happen like that. But he didn't want to take the chance.

'You sa'ed that boy's life,' Trevor Brown had said in the park.

Not yet, thought Socrates. *Not yet.*

His mother entered in a dream. She was older but still standing straight and tall. They were in the small front room in the house in Cartersville. The picture window looked out over a field of jagged stumps of cornstalks.

Socrates sat at a small table that had a fancy linen cloth across it. He was looking at his big hands while she stood next to the window that was filled with blue sky and the field of corn. The sun was so bright through the window that Mrs Fortlow seemed to be in a shadow.

Socrates couldn't even see her eyes.

'What?' he asked, almost angry. He realized that he was in a conversation that had been going on for years. 'What?'

There was no answer.

Socrates was going to rise. He was going to get up and make her understand how bad he felt. But he couldn't get up; he couldn't even lift his hands off the table.

He felt so weak that he started crying. And

while he cried his waking mind wondered how many times had he sat before that blue window, and his mother – crying?

Then she moved.

He was sure that this had never happened before.

Another step, and he remembered all the times that he just wanted to say that he was sorry for the happiness he had taken from her.

Another step and he could see her eyes. They were pleading, crying without tears. No words came from her wet lips.

'What?' Socrates asked again.

He lifted his hands. Somehow this changed things and she was gone. All that was left was his chair and the window full of sky and corn. Socrates had gotten smaller and smaller. Now he was no more than an ant peeking over the sill into a world larger than he could imagine.

'No.'

'Momma.'

'Uh-uh, no. Stop it.'

Socrates opened his eyes.

'No,' said Darryl from his sleep in the other room.

Socrates sat next to the foldout sofa bed. He didn't touch Darryl or try to wake him up. He'd been taught when he was a child that a man's dreams were private – like sex or going to the bathroom – and should never be interrupted.

So Socrates sat for an hour or so, until the shifting, moaning boy's eyes snapped open.

'Hey,' he said to the big man.

'Hey.'

'I'ont know if I could take this,' Darryl said.

'You don't know if you could take what?'

'I dreamed that instead'a you gettin' there in time Philip shot me in the head. An' an' an' an' Yvette Frank was right there but I'as too afraid to get my dick hard because I was dead.'

Socrates laughed knowingly. Then he said, 'Don't you worry, boy. I'm always gonna be there on time.'

Darryl blinked once and turned over on his side. He was asleep in an instant and Socrates wondered if the boy had ever been awake.

4

'But he cain't stay down here no more,' Socrates said to Luvia Prine. Right Burke, Luvia's handicapped roomer and Socrates' best friend, was sitting between them. Darryl was out in the kitchen making M&M cookies with Luvia's niece, Willomena.

'Why not?' Luvia didn't like Socrates but she liked his friends. She cared about Darryl and didn't even chastise Right for going over, now

170

and then, to see how the man and boy were doing.

'You know how these gangster kids is,' Socrates said. 'They gonna get him on a drive-by or make him join up. You know how it is.'

'Let him go home to his momma then,' Luvia said. She stood up to show that the problem was settled and over.

'He ain't got no daddy at home an' that neighborhood his momma in is right in the middle'a all that shit,' little Right said. He knew that the only way to get Luvia back in her seat was if he showed that he was worried too. 'Darryl's momma let him stay wit' Socco because she knew he needed someone with a strong hand to help out. But even Socco cain't be there every minute.'

'What can I do about that, Mr Burke?' the skinny, tall, hard-boned woman asked. 'You know my house is for retired people like you an' Mrs Halloway an' them. We cain't have no boys runnin' wild in the halls.'

'They's the MacDanielses,' Right whispered.

Socrates was so nervous that he blinked.

Luvia froze in mid-gesture. Her hand had been reaching – maybe for an itch on her cheek – but it stayed there suspended a few inches from her face.

'You know you should be ashamed to let them words out your mouth, Right Burke,' Luvia said at last. 'You know it's a sin what you said.'

'It's hard,' the WWII veteran agreed. He lifted

171

his mangled left hand in a gesture that was indecipherable. 'But it ain't no sin. Hallie an' Costas lost a boy to the street; they lost Bernard. Now here comes a chance for them to do somethin' about it.'

'That's exactly right,' Socrates said, feeling that they were the truest words that he had ever spoken.

'I might have to listen to Mr Burke, Socrates Fortlow,' Luvia said. 'But that don't mean I have to hear you.'

'I know, Luvia,' Socrates said, smiling. 'You don't like the way I smell an' I ain't even took off my shoe . . .'

Right chuckled.

Socrates went on, '. . . an' you ain't wrong neither. Naw, you ain't wrong. But this ain't between you'n me. This here is about a boy that's gonna die . . .'

Luvia put both of her hands up, like stop signs. 'I don't know if you're right or wrong but that don't matter. I cain't be askin' Hallie an' Costas to be takin' in nobody. They just buried Bernard, they grievin'. An' they cain't be takin' care'a nobody new after all them doctor bills an' the funeral . . .'

Bernard had been shot down at a house in View Park. He'd been cruising with some friends. They had words with another group of children. Shots were fired later on that night, at a party. Bernard didn't die at first; for about a week the doctors thought that he might survive. But then he just lost the will to live. A fever, like fire, had burned out his life on the eighth day after the shooting.

'I take home one fifty-nine thirty-five in a week,' Socrates said. 'An' I get maybe seventy-five in tips from home deliveries on top'a that. All my tips could go to Darryl. And he got him a job down at Bounty, so he don't need no allowance. Between him an' me we could pay for him t'stay with them.'

Luvia sagged in her chair. Her stiff backbone couldn't take Socrates' weight. Her eyes hated him more and more.

'What good it gonna do to have Darryl over there?' she pleaded with Right.

'It's another school for him, Miss Prine. And they way over there near Hauser an' Venice. Darryl'd have a chance over there. You know a boy tryin' deserves a chance.'

'But how could I ask Hallie to do that?' Luvia asked either man.

'Just ask'em. Just ask. Maybe they need another chance,' Right said.

Socrates had been biting the inside of his cheek. Suddenly he felt his mouth fill with blood. He swallowed hard, swallowed again, and then nodded. Hallie and Costas MacDaniels were staunch churchgoers. They believed in the Lord and the Lord's righteous representatives; these didn't include the whiskey-breathed Right and certainly not a convicted murderer like Socrates Fortlow.

'Okay,' Luvia said, standing again. 'I guess I could ask'em.'

Right yipped and hollered. He jumped up out of his chair and hugged Luvia. Because he was so much shorter his head was up hard against her breast. While trying to push him back she eyed Socrates.

He had a big, lippy grin on his face. He didn't laugh because he didn't want to change Luvia's mind with a show of bloody teeth.

'What you laughin' at, Socrates Fortlow?'

He shook his head and kept smiling – swallowing blood all the while.

5

'But what if I don't wanna go?' Darryl asked a week later. The MacDanielses had said yes to taking him in even before they met him. Luvia had told them everything she could to dissuade them but all they could think of was helping that boy.

'Luvia tells us that you had some troubles with the police in the past,' Costas MacDaniels said when they met in Socrates' small rooms.

'I was in prison, sir,' Socrates said, on his best behavior.

'Oh,' said Mrs MacDaniels.

She was plum-shaped and plum-colored. They were both tiny. But his voice was like a tuba where hers was no more than the tinkle of a triangle.

'Such a Christian man,' Hallie said. 'You must be very close to God to work so hard to help young Darryl.'

Socrates smiled and nodded a lot. The MacDanielses said that he could come by to see Darryl anytime he wanted. They preferred that Darryl stay away from Watts.

Socrates smiled and nodded. He didn't like Hallie and Costas. They were cowed and cowardly, he thought. But he also loved them because they had the power to do what he could not.

'You makin' me go because'a what happened in the park,' Darryl said. ''Cause you're mad.'

'You did fine in the park. Like I said, you did your best.'

'I mean 'cause I was gonna shoot Philip – that's why, huh? You mad 'cause you think it's wrong for black people t'kill each other but I almost did.'

'No,' Socrates said, nonchalant. 'That boy humiliated you, beat you, tried to kill you. I'ont even think a white man's court could find you guilty over all that.'

'But then why you make me drop the gun?'

''Cause you don't know how to shoot. You prob'ly woulda shot some innocent bystander. That wouldn't be good, now would it?'

'I wanna stay here wit' you,' Darryl answered.

'You gonna see me ev'ry day, almost, at the supermarket. I'll come an' visit you at the MacDanielses' an' you could come on down

175

here whenever you want. Don't worry, Darryl, this here's gonna be good for you. It's gonna be good. I want you there, your momma wants you there, the MacDanielses want you there. Only ones that want you down here is Philip an' his wolf pack. That's all that want you here.'

Darryl nodded and hugged his big friend. When the MacDaniels came to take him away he cried.

'I never seen'im cry before,' Socrates was telling Right later that night. They were chipping away at a cheap fifth of PM whiskey. 'I know it gotta be good if he could cry.'

'Yep,' Right said. He was so drunk that he wavered in his chair. 'Boy cried.'

'An' it's good for me too,' Socrates added. 'You know it could get cramped wit' two people up in here.'

'Yep.' Right nodded. 'Yep, yep.'

'Can you make it home, Right?' Socrates asked.

Right looked up from his Dixie cup and blinked once, then once again. 'Nope,' he said.

'That's okay, old man,' Socrates said, laughing. 'You take my bed. Go on now, 'fore you fall on the floor.'

Mrs Irene Fortlow walked all the way to Socrates, as he sat at the small table in the little front room, in Cartersville. The sky was blue in the picture window and the corn was green. He put his big arms around her waist and laid his head against

176

her breast. When she caressed his head he fell into a deep sleep – not waking until morning.

The streets were as noisy as ever, filled with booming radios from passing cars, police sirens, and loud talk, but still it was the best sleep that he could remember.

LETTER TO THERESA

1

Socrates had been sick for three days. It was the intestinal flu and it was bad. His stomach rejected everything, even water. He lay back in his foldout sofa bed dehydrated and feverish, worried that they'd fire him from his job at Bounty Supermarket just because he didn't have a phone and couldn't call in sick. There was a pay phone three blocks away but he hardly had the strength to make it from one room to the other.

The first two days he forced himself from the bed to drink water and urinate. But by day three he had cracked lips and a dry tongue; he couldn't even think about moving without getting dizzy. He would have wet his bed except for the fact that there was nothing left in him to wet with.

Nobody dropped by to visit and Socrates rued anew that he had no phone. He knew that he was dying for lack of a friend to hear his call.

Mostly he slept, dreaming about prison and childhood friends. He dreamed about his mother too. Her strong voice echoing down the empty gray cellblock, calling to him from the grave.

On the afternoon of the third day Socrates opened his eyes but was still dreaming.

Theresa stood there at the foot of the bed. He wouldn't have come awake then even if Warden Johns came down and demanded it; even if God called Judgment Day with his great golden hammer.

'Theresa?'

'Yeah, baby?'

At the sound of her voice he was a young man again come home from a beating. He couldn't remember why he caught such hell. He didn't even remember who he'd been fighting.

But Theresa didn't ask. She cradled him in her lap and put a wet towel on his forehead. She put a hand against his chest while the cold tendrils of water trickled down his neck and shoulders.

'Shh,' she whispered.

'Baby.'

'Shh.'

When he woke up he was still dreaming. Theresa was waiting for him and his cuts were bandaged.

'Hi, baby,' she said.

He remembered her in tan slacks and one of his torn T-shirts. Her face was like a mirror, every cut and bruise reflected in her concerned eye.

'I'm sorry, T,' he said.

'When you gonna stop doin' like this, Socrates?'

'I don't know.'

Something snapped or cracked or fell down in the other room but Socrates held Theresa's eye.

'Because,' she said. 'Because I cain't always be fixin' you up. I cain't spend my whole life worryin' about you.'

The pain in his head came from words he couldn't get out. They pounded against the inside of his skull. He tried to wet his tongue to say something but there was no saliva.

'Don't go' died in his throat.

2

'What's that you said, Socco?' Darryl asked. 'Huh?'

The skinny boy was at the foot of the bed where Theresa had been standing.

'Pour some water on my head, Darryl.'

'What?'

'Pour some water on my head.'

After some coaxing Darryl poured water from a gallon pail over Socrates' shoulders, neck, and head. The ex-con leaned over the side of the bed so as not to wet his mattress. He moaned loudly as the cold water rushed over his fevered skin and onto the concrete floor.

Darryl went out for aspirin and broth. He fed Socrates by hand for two days.

'Where you learn how to take care'a a sick man?' Socrates asked when he was on the mend.

'My momma took care'a me, ain't she?' the boy responded.

Sol Epstein was happy to see Socrates back on the job.

'When you're around everybody seems to work harder,' the assistant manager at Bounty Super-market said.

He believed that Socrates had been sick. He even authorized sick pay for the time that Socrates was out.

For days Socrates worked, wondering when was the last time he felt so healthy and well. He slept soundly each night but still he felt as if he had been aware so that if somebody came into the room he would have known it just as if he were awake, with his eyes open.

On his first day off he woke up early and went to the table in the kitchen. He began writing a letter in pencil on a pad of Holiday Inn notepaper that he'd bought secondhand at the army surplus store.

3

'Dear Theresa,' the letter began. 'I saw you in a dream the other night and so I wanted to say hay.'

For the next hour he sat there reading and rereading his sentence. It was all true but it didn't go anywhere. He couldn't talk about the flu and the pain in his head, about Darryl and the water. He didn't want to sound sickly and asking for help. If he saw her it would be okay, she'd see that he was independent now.

'I guess I want to see you,' he wrote. 'I do want to see you. And then I could tell you about prison and how you were right. I know you probably married and got a lotta kids by now . . .'

Socrates stopped again. Reread again. He wondered if he knew her husband. He wondered how old her kids were. He counted up the years. Thirty-five. One when she was still writing him in jail and then another a year later. Maybe as many as twelve. Her oldest child would be in his thirties. The youngest no younger than twenty-three.

'. . . grandchildren too probably. I miss you, T. I almost died from flu and I thought about you. You was always asking when was I going to stop being so crazy. I never said nothing to that because I didn't want to be lying. You know I wanted to stop. But what if I said I would and then I didn't?

'I stopped now. I been out of prison eight years and more. I been solid. I got a job and an apartment. I got friends and there is this teenage boy I been helping. I know you married. T. I know that because you wanted it and you always did what you wanted to do.

'I remember when you took me up to your father's grave at Haven Home. I remember you said he was laying in the ground but he was still more man than most of these niggers walking around on two legs. I remember that. I know you did not mean me but even still it was about me anyway.

'But I am not like that anymore. I can take care of myself now. I don't get into trouble even when it's not my fault.

'I would like to hear from you, T. Just two friends talking. I will put my address down bottom. If you get this letter and you want to write then you can.'

Socrates signed the notepaper and wrote down his address. He sent it from the main post office at Florence and Central. He remembered Theresa's mother's address because her mother's name was Rose and Rose lived on 32 Rose Street.

4

Sylvia Marquette had a little store that dealt mainly in candy bars and soda pop, potato chips and beer. But at the back, behind the stand-alone cooler, she kept a block of copper mailboxes.

Sylvia's market was Socrates' mailing address.

'No, Mr Fortlow,' Sylvia said. 'Ain't no mail for you. No.'

Her face was squashed in on itself. No forehead to speak of and little chin. She was quite dark except for her eyes. The whites of the ugly woman's eyes were like hundred-watt bulbs.

'Why you comin' in here every day, Mr Fortlow? I used to only see you once a week.'

'Expectin' a letter,' he said.

'A check?' Sylvia's eyes increased their voltage.

'Old girlfriend,' he said.

'Oh,' the shopkeeper cooed. Her voice had become low, and very sexy. 'That stuff is better'n money sometimes; 'cept if you hungry.'

''Cept if she gone,' Socrates added.

They both laughed hard.

'All right then,' Socrates said, concluding their play. 'I'll see ya tomorrah.'

'Good seein' you anytime, Mr Fortlow.' Sylvia's voice was sincere.

Socrates was feeling good as he left the little store even though he'd come to realize over the four weeks since he'd sent his letter that Theresa was gone from him forever – again.

In his sleep Sylvia was still laughing. But instead of a happy friend she sounded like a cartoon witch, cackling and savoring his pain. Her hot coughs battered against his eardrums and soured his stomach. In the middle of the night Socrates woke up feeling as if the flu had returned.

If he stayed awake he was okay. But if he dozed, or even lay down, the laughing returned and with it the sick stomach.

'You should take the day off, Mr Fortlow. You look bad,' Sol Epstein said. There was concern in his wrinkled white face.

'Naw, man. No. Lemme do another shift.'

'Another shift? You look like you should be in the hospital.'

'I can't sleep, Mr Epstein. Maybe if I work two shifts I'll be tired enough to go to bed.'

'What's wrong?' the daytime manager asked.

'It's these dreams, man. Not dreams really but like things I see and hear in my sleep.'

Sol Epstein was a short man, strong on top and fat underneath. His hair was the kind of gray that seemed to be blue. He had the cruel slate-gray eyes of a task-master but his smile, when he smiled, made him a kind uncle.

He smiled then.

'You might need some help, Socrates.'

'What kinda help?'

'Counselor. Psychologist. Somethin' like that.'

'Shit. Only counselin' I need is to work my butt off until I cain't see straight no more. That's what I need.' Socrates was thinking about the prison psychiatrist. All he'd done was to give tests with circles and squares on them, that and pass out drugs.

'Can I stay?' Socrates asked.

'Sure,' said the kind uncle.

5

He worked seven shifts in four days and stopped picking up the mail from Sylvia Marquette. He drank a half pint of whiskey while listening to the cool jazz radio station every night.

Nothing helped.

He couldn't sleep.

He was losing weight and his hearing had turned strange. Sounds had become louder, tinny. Sometimes he didn't hear what people said at all. Whenever anyone spoke to him it seemed as if they were speaking Chinese or some other foreign language.

He looked older in the mirror, and for the first time in his life he felt weak in his arms and hands. He knew that he couldn't win a fight with his hands and so he started carrying a knife again and listening closer to the foreign language that everyone around him was speaking.

He was listening for threatening tones.

One day he was watching Sol Epstein from the back of the store. Sol was giving his kind-uncle smile to Noah Hoag, a young boxboy. Socrates remembered Sol's advice to him about a counselor. He knew that it was his only chance.

The next day Socrates took out his delivery push wagon. He dropped off groceries for Watson, Kirkaby, and Stein. Eight seventy-five in tips. Then he went down the long Beverly Hills alley that was better paved and maintained than most of the streets in Watts. He passed behind a house that was on Chaldy Lane and quickly pushed his cart through a redwood doorway parking it behind a stand of rose bushes.

He knocked on Mrs Hampton's back door but

he knew that she was in Miami visiting her dying sister. He put on his work gloves, took the key from the light fixture over the door, and let himself into the small house.

White walls trimmed with green and dark wood furniture decorated every room. Small photographs of relatives stood on each windowsill. The smell in the cool air was faint and sweet.

Socrates delivered a brisket roast or two small chickens, bell peppers, potatoes, and frozen containers of diet lemonade to Mrs Hampton every Tuesday. Sometimes she'd call in to add to that order. She'd told him about the key for days when she was out. And if she was out there was always a four-dollar tip waiting for him on the dinette table next to the phone.

There was no tip today. Socrates sat at the table and peered through lace curtains out onto Chaldy Lane. A horn tooted somewhere and Socrates realized how quiet it was in that house. No one talking, no loud banging.

You only had to remember the exchange to dial this number because the last four digits were the letters G-I-R-L.

'Girls,' a pleasant woman's voice said. 'What kind of girl do you want, sir? Blond, brunette, Asian baby?'

'I wanna talk to Theresa,' Socrates said.

The pleasant voice hesitated a moment. Maybe she heard the deep violence and despair in him.

'Just a moment,' she said.

The phone clicked and there was dead silence. After a few seconds Socrates began to wonder if they had hung up.

'Hello?' It was a black woman's voice.

'Theresa?'

Another hesitation and then, 'Yeah. Who's this?'

'It's Socrates.'

'Oh hi, Socrates,' she said, loud and happy, it seemed, to hear an old friend. 'What do you want me to do for you? You wanna hear what I got on?'

'How are you, Theresa?'

'I'm fine. Real fine.'

'Uh-huh. You know it's been a while.'

'Yeah,' the woman answered, her voice more subdued. 'What is it you want from me, Mr Socrates?'

'I just want some talk is all.'

'Talk about what?' she asked, hardly pleasant at all.

'I wanna talk to Theresa.'

'And what is it you need to say to me?'

'Are you Theresa?'

'I am right now. Yeah. Now what did you have to say? Because you know I cain't be listenin' to no weird shit, baby.'

'It's just been a long time an' I wanna catch up. That's all.'

'You been sick?' Telephone Theresa asked.

Socrates coughed out a harsh laugh. 'Yeah. That

188

was the last thing on a whole line'a things. I was sick an' I dreamed about you.'

'What was I wearin'?' she asked.

'You had on them tan slacks and that ole T-shirt'a mine. I was all beat up and you put a cold towel on my head.' Tears were coming from Socrates' eyes but he kept the crying out of his voice.

'Uh-huh,' the woman said. 'What else?'

'I don't get in trouble like that anymore. I don't get into fights every night. I only drink in my house sometimes. You know I learned some things, Theresa. I'm outta jail and I ain't goin' back there no more.'

'Yeah, baby, that's good,' the woman answered. 'What you wanna do now that you outta jail? You missed bein' with a woman when you was in there?'

'The first few years it was hard but not no more. I got it now. You know I figgered out that livin' is kinda like music. You know what I mean? Like when you walk, you know. Ev'ry step is the same length and takes the same amount'a time. An' your heart too. Even your eyes blinkin' is pretty much the same beat unless somethin' messes up. Maybe somethin' gets in your eye or you gotta run . . .'

Telephone Theresa made the quick hollow breath of half-yawn but Socrates didn't care.

He went on, '. . . an' if you could keep up that beat they ain't no reason t'be drunk or mad.'

'How long were you in jail?' Theresa asked.

'Twenty-seven years.'

'And did you miss your girl all that time?'

'I thought about you every night. I knew you were right. I knew that I did wrong. But it was like I couldn't help it. I thought about all the children and good times and even the bad times we coulda had. Maybe I'da got fat and lazy drinkin' beer on the front porch while you was on the phone to your girlfriends and yellin' at the kids to stop all that horseplay. I thought about it so much that I prob'ly lived it more than if I was free.'

'Did you miss my body?' the woman asked.

'Yes,' he whispered. 'Yes I did.'

'Would you lay up in that cot at night holdin' on to yo'self an' thinkin' how you wanted me to kiss it?'

Socrates nodded.

'Huh?' she asked.

'Yes.'

''Cause that's what I wanted, baby. I missed that hard dick you got for me. I was thinkin' about that. I wanted you to fuck me with that.'

Another horn honked in the street. Weeks later when Socrates was telling Right Burke about what a crazy fool he had been, breaking into Mrs Hampton's house and trying to call *the woman of his dreams*, he remembered that horn.

'It was Telephone Theresa's dirty talk and that horn,' Socrates said to Right at a checkers table in McKinley Park. 'That made me wake up.'

'Wake up?' the maimed vet said. 'You was sleepwalkin'?'

190

'Yup. Ever since I had that flu I been in a dream. She was so real, man. I believed that I saw her. I even tried to write. Here I ain't spoke to her in thirty-fi'e years an' I'm tryin' t'write her a letter, tryin' t'call her on the phone.'

'Damn,' Right said, rubbing his chin with his paralyzed claw. 'You was way out there, huh? Did you really think that that was your old girlfriend on the phone?'

'I wanted it to be, Right. I wanted to pretend so much that maybe a little bit I thought it was real. But then when that girl started to get my dick hard I knew I couldn't pretend no more. The woman I wanted was gone. Gone.'

6

A month passed. Socrates had settled back down into his routine. He slept every night straight through, getting up only twice to go to the toilet.

Mrs Hampton didn't seem to suspect him of breaking in and using her phone. Maybe she was so rich that the ten or twelve dollars just slipped by her. Maybe she complained and the telephone company let it go.

Darryl was growing every day. His voice got deeper and his walk became graceful. He was doing the push ups that Socrates had showed him and his arms grew thicker and firm.

★   ★   ★

Socrates was coming home from work one day when a woman called out to him, 'Mr Fortlow! Socrates! Hey!'

Sylvia Marquette came up to him. The full sun on Central Avenue did not, in any way, dim the brightness of her eyes.

'You ain't been by in six weeks, Mr Fortlow,' she said.

'No,' Socrates agreed.

Something about the woman still disturbed him. Her squashed-down face, the hairs that sprouted from a black mole on her right cheek.

'You got that letter,' she said.

Dear Mr Fortlow,

It's been many years since I even thought your name. For a long time I hoped that I would never hear of you again and, God forgive me, sometimes I even hoped that you'd never get out o that jail. But your letter touched my heart and I finally thought to write and answer your questions. I'm sorry that it has taken so long but I'm blind now and I had to wait for my granddaughter, Cova, to come by and read your letter to me.

My daughter, Theresa, married Criston Jones in 1961. They gave me four beautiful grandchildren (including Cova, who is writing this letter) and then moved to Los Angeles. They had four more children out there. Criston worked at McDonnell Douglas for many years and then he died from diabetes. Criston was a healthy eater but his bones and organs just couldn't take all that weight.

Theresa saw her last baby, Teju, through college and then she collapsed from all that work. She was admitted to Falana Rest Home on Criston's health insurance but she never recovered. Theresa Childress-Jones died on November third of last year. She is survived by Malcolm, Cova, Mister, Sandy, Criston Jr, Minnie, Lana, and Teju. All of her children are healthy and well. Most of them have good jobs, though Teju and Lana have become artists.

I know that you cared for my daughter, Mr Fortlow, and I'll tell you that Theresa lived a good life. She was happy and rich in love. I never heard her say a harsh word about you and I know it broke her heart to see you go to jail.

Theresa Childress-Jones is buried at Valley Rest in Pomona next to her husband. There's a plot to her left for me, Mr Fortlow. I'm eighty-four and so I'll probably be coming out to rest next to my daughter before too long.

I'm glad that you've found some peace, Mr Fortlow. I know that Theresa would have been glad too.

Sincerely yours,
Rose Childress

It took three and a half hours by bus to get to Valley Rest. Socrates got there on an overcast and warm afternoon. Her slender marble headstone stood elegant and straight next to Criston's. His stone was wider and not quite as tall.

On each stone there was merely a name and the dates.

Socrates wanted more.

He wanted an address and a phone number; an invitation to her house when everybody was there for the Fourth of July. He wanted Nat King Cole on the record player playing out of the window and a cold beer on the patio with the both of them. Him and Criston talking about work and where they came from in Indiana; Theresa calling the children over one by one to meet the man who could have been their father.

He would have been standing right there on that spot for Criston's funeral. Theresa would be vulnerable but he wouldn't take advantage of her. He'd offer consoling talk, money, or to fix things around the house. He'd hold her hand and tell her that she had eight kids and one old friend who needed her not to die.

He wanted to take her back to Rose on Rose Street.

He wanted, for the first time since he was young, to go back home. He could have walked with her down Rose to Thatcher and down Thatcher to Thirty-Second Street just to see where the streetcars used to run with an old friend who had forgiven him.

He wanted to hear that forgiveness.

Socrates stared at the graves for over an hour,

wanting; his jaw clenched to keep from shouting at the stones. His heart beat erratically and fast. In prison he had learned to live without desire. And now that he had let desire in he wanted everything.

All that wanting wore on him until the only desire left was to lie down and sleep on Theresa's grave. But he knew that it was wrong. He knew, beyond that, that it was probably against the rules.

He stood there wavering over the grave.

'Hey, mister,' a voice said.

He was a small black man dressed in a too warm brown suit and wearing a short-brimmed hat. He might have been Socrates' age but looked older, more resigned.

'Yeah?' Socrates said.

'These your people?' the man asked.

Socrates nodded slightly.

The man peered at the stones mumbling numbers on his lips. Socrates realized that he was figuring out their ages.

'It's a shame how so many black folks die so young,' the man said.

'Oh, I don't know,' Socrates said loudly. The trees shimmered green and silver under pearl-gray skies. 'I think a whole lotta our people put more into a year than some others might do. Sometimes it just takes a hour and you done had a lifetime.'

HISTORY

0

Socrates stayed in his house for three days watching the tiny black-and-white TV screen. He turned the volume off after the first few moments of coverage. There were mainly aerial shots of the blocks burning around him. That and the continual video replay of some white man being dragged from a truck and beaten by raging black men.

He stayed in his tiny rooms, eating boiled rice and tuna sandwiches, but Socrates wasn't afraid of the riot; not, at least, of any harm that might befall him. Any harm in Mr Forlow's vicinity would fall upon somebody else – that's why he stayed inside.

He'd served up Molotov cocktails every night in his prison dreams. He broke white flesh with his fists and laughed as the cellblock collapsed.

In prison he prayed for his door to spring open and a riot to be waiting outside. He would have been willing to die.

The smoke coming through the cracks in his

apartment walls smelled of sweet revenge. Every scar on his body and curse in his ear, every sour stomach and sleepless night, every minute in prison, every white girl on a magazine cover, every image in his mind for twenty-seven years of incarceration wanted out in that street.

But Socrates stayed inside refusing to ball up his fists. He heard the mobs roaming the streets through his thin walls. He watched them, on the mute TV, living out his dreams.

On the third day he saw the snowy image of a billboard falling from its high perch. He wasn't sure but then they replayed the footage on Channel 13 half an hour later. The sign said HARPO'S BAZAAR. He knew that sign. He knew that there was only one place for it to fall.

Socrates forgot the TV after that. The images played on but Socrates was remembering back several years, back when he had just gotten out of jail.

Those days he spent roaming the streets; a free man after all those years locked away. He was waiting for somebody to give him a look so he could break their face for them. Whenever he'd see a young woman in short pants and halter top he'd taste whatever it was that he'd eaten last. The twisted face from his sour stomach would scare all the women away from him, and somewhere, inside, he was relieved.

He knew that he was on a path to violence.

He knew that he'd die before they got him back in the cage.

He was counting the days so he would know in that final moment how long he'd made it before they cut him down.

And then, on day sixty-two, he walked past Harpo's Bazaar, a secondhand store on Martin Luther King Jr Boulevard. Next door was the Canyon minimall. There were only two businesses open out of the five stores, Lucky Liquors and the Capricorn Bookshop.

Socrates bought a half pint of Apache Gin and walked into the bookstore because he hoped that they had air conditioning.

Capricorn was on his route then. He was no longer roaming. He had a place to go.

As the riots raged outside his walls, Socrates remembered the little bookstore and the men and women who despised and loved him.

1

'I don't like you, Socrates Fortlow,' Roland Winters had said. He was pudgy and small, a bespectacled man with strawberry-brown skin. 'You, an' people like you, the whole reason we got so much heartache down here. Always thinkin' violence; always wantin' ta beat on, never wantin' to get on your knees to God.'

Socrates hadn't been out of prison for very long,

sixty-two days and four weeks. He'd come to the bookstore because you could sit around there and nobody asked you to buy anything or to leave. He could read all day and even talk to other *customers* who sat along the reading shelf.

Roland sat in a shaft of green light that shone through the tinted front window of the Capricorn Bookshop. Mrs Minette, the owner, sat behind her cash register smiling sweetly just as if the men seated at her reading table were trading compliments.

The hot promise of a slap jerked in Socrates' right palm. He held back though – not because he thought it was wrong to hit Roland but because he wanted to be welcome at the Capricorn. He liked browsing through the Afro-American literature and talking to Mr and Mrs Minette about what he read.

Black cowboys running roughshod in Oklahoma. Black scientists and war heroes and con men. He liked the smell of the Minettes' incense and the promise of things that he never even suspected were true.

'Oh, Roland, shut up,' Minty Seale said. 'Just shet it. All Socco did was ask a question. He ain't even ask you.'

'I don't have to be quiet if I don't wanna be,' Roland complained. 'He could ask a question an' I could speak my mind.'

A lazy smile rippled across Minty's big lips. He was a long-boned man, thirty-five, a wallpaperer by profession, and unemployed. Socrates thought that Minty was trying to fire Roland up rather than calm him down.

'I'ont need your help, Minty,' the big ex-convict said. 'I could take care'a myself.'

'No, Socco,' the fourth man at the long counter said. 'It wouldn'ta made no difference if the African people had gunpowder. Africans just wasn't warlike – not like them Europeans. Chinese neither, they had ignitin' powder for a thousand years an' they never done nuthin' with it like Europe did.'

The last man was only known as Big Bill. He weighed nearly four hundred pounds and had to sit on a box instead of a folding chair. He had a job with a real estate agency on Avalon and drove a 1969 Impala that was pink and chrome – in beautiful condition.

'China!' Roland yelled. 'China got guns. They got guns and cannon – an' the atomic bomb! That's what men like this one here,' Roland waved dismissively at Socrates, 'don't know about, or don't care. You start talkin' guns an' it all just escalates. From fists to guns, from guns to dynamite, from dynamite to the atomic bomb.'

'The atomic bomb?' Minty said. 'The atomic bomb? Don't tell me them folks down at the federal buildin' got you fooled, Roland. The atomic bomb? Shoot! That's just some lie that they tellin' to keep people in line. They tell you they got some bomb so bad that you better not ever even think about tryin' to get what's yours. That's how they keep people down – wit' lies like the atomic bomb.'

Minty turned his chair around so that he could look down the row of men. When he put his big bare feet up on the table Mrs Minette frowned. Minty, and everybody else, knew that she didn't like feet up on her furniture, but she would never interrupt an intellectual conversation to say so.

'Aw, com'on, Minty,' Big Bill said. 'You ain't sayin' that you don't believe in nuclear power.'

'I'm not, huh? You used to watch Walter Cronkite back in 'sixty-four, 'sixty-five?' Minty asked Bill.

'Yeah?'

'Me too. Ev'ry night I be sittin' there lookin' to see if they'd show a picture of my brother Doren over there in Vietnam. You know I'as only twelve, thirteen but I knew that ole Walt was lyin' like a motherfucker.'

'What?'

'Lyin', man. Five hunnert VC killed; one American wounded. Next day – two thousand North Vietnamese regulars routed with only three Americans killed. Shit! You add up all that at the end'a the war an' we done killed over half'a Asia – forget about Vietnam.'

'But that was war, Minty,' Bill said. 'They lie like that durin' a war to keep up confidence at home.'

'This is a war,' Socrates said. He was angry at himself for talking so softly but he was intimidated by how intelligent the men at Capricorn sounded. They were so confident about their words.

'What, Socco?' Minty asked. There was a big grin on his lips.

'That's what you sayin', right, Minty? That we're in a war against them men own ev'rything. The newspapers, the TV stations, the army, and the police. They tell us what they want us to know. If it's a lie then it is, but if it's the truth it don't matter because they only say it 'cause it helps them out.' Socrates felt a film of sweat form across his bald head. He wasn't a timid man and he was willing to put his life on the line where most men would have run scared. But he was shy of the men and women at the Capricorn because they were readers. No prison-yard lawyers or bullshitters. These people studied the history of black folks because they loved to learn.

'There you go again,' Roland chirped. 'Talkin' war, talkin' violence, talkin' 'bout how it's somebody else fault. Say what you want but God know that it's on you. When the judgment come he ain't gonna take no excuse. You cain't be sayin' that it's the newspaper fault 'cause you shot that man. You cain't say it's the girly magazine made you rape that woman.' The little man slapped his belly as if he had a round drum wrapped up in his T-shirt.

'Let him talk, Roland.' Her soft voice was ethereal, like the voice of ghosts in old black-and-white movies.

The men all turned. It was unusual for Mrs.

Minette to get involved in the talks that went on in her store. It was said that she was ten years younger than her husband – who was eighty-five – but she didn't even look fifty. She sat behind her desk all day, smiling and talking little. Mrs Minette ran the store, which was little more than a big empty room with bookshelves along the walls and the slender reading table across the front window.

'His kinda talk is wrong, Winifred,' Roland said.

Winifred. Socrates mouthed the name.

'Anybody can say what they want here,' she whispered. 'What were you saying, Mr Fortlow?'

'Uh . . . I wasn't sayin' nuthin' really.' He was a convict again, lying to a guard. 'Minty and Bill was just sayin', they was just sayin' that it's a war of lies that we're in.'

'A war of lies?' Mrs Minette spoke and held her head the way she did when she was talking to the children who came to the after-school day care program that the bookstore ran.

Socrates didn't mind her condescension.

'Yeah,' he said. 'That's what Minty meant. He meant that almost ev'rything we hear is a lie or, even worse, just half' a what's true. That's why me an' an' an' uh me an' Roland get so mad . . .'

'Why's that?' Mr Oscar Minette asked. Socrates hadn't even heard the bell on the front door.

'Hi,' Winifred Minette said to her husband.

Socrates imagined all of the sweet knowledge buried in her hello. It made him happy.

'Hey, Mr Minette,' Minty said as he removed his feet from the table. 'How you doin'?'

'Oscar,' said Bill in way of a greeting.

Mr Minette was tall, thin, and lame. He had on a fuzzy gray suit with a chocolate-brown rayon shirt underneath. His cane was brown and so were his shoes.

Mr Minette bowed to each of the men and then asked again, 'What were you going to say, Mr Fortlow?'

2

Socrates stared at Mr Minette. He understood the question but didn't think about an answer. He knew the answer but somehow that didn't seem to matter. He felt like a boy in school. He was in awe that he was picked out to speak.

Call on me, Socrates remembered shouting with his arm held up so stiffly that it shook. *Call on me.*

Oscar Minette limped across the big room, slowly approaching his wife. She turned her smooth round cheek to him, he kissed it, then she stood on her toes to kiss him.

Bill jumped up, grabbing a folding chair from behind the desk, then shaking it out for the elder. But Mr Minette didn't sit. He stood behind the chair, holding it to steady himself.

'What did you say, Socrates?'

'That Roland an' me always fightin' because we

204

cain't believe in what we sayin' to each other.' Socrates heard the words as they came out of his mouth. They sounded good, maybe even true. Twenty-three years angry and poor, twenty-seven more in prison, and then all of a sudden it just all fell into place. 'They lyin' to us so much that we always lookin' for the trick behind what they sayin'. 'Cause there's always a trick, even if you don't think there is.'

'I'idn't say nuthin' like that,' Roland Winters said. 'I said I don't like you because you don't accept God. 'Cause you always talkin' 'bout crooks like that George Washington Williams, an' cowboys, an' guns.'

Socrates didn't want to slap Roland anymore. He didn't want to hurt anybody for the first time that he could remember.

'Ain't it Christian to forgive an' to teach?' Minty asked. He was still grinning, still jabbing the needle.

Oscar Minette beamed at Socrates; Winifred smiled at her husband. Roland was quiet while Minty grinned at him; Big Bill didn't seem to know what to do with his hands.

It was still all so clear to Socrates while the riots raged outside, years later, the picture of his first friends outside of prison. The smell of incense. The radio playing low in the cabinet under Mrs Minette's cash register.

'There's always a trick,' Socrates repeated. 'Man tells another one to believe in something because he believes it; later on he finds out that he was wrong. Boy tells a girl that he loves her but when he gets what he really wanted he see that he don't even like her. An' then he blames her for burnin' the food or spendin' too much time with her friends.'

Oscar Minette nodded.

'It's a lie when a black man open his mouth,' Socrates said. 'An' he know it too. That's why if a black man lucky enough to live till he old he don't have much to say. *I'm hungry, I tired*, that's just about all that ain't some lie.'

Roland left. He never stayed in the store long whenever Socrates was around after that day. Minty put on his shoes and went too. He had a date, Socrates remembered, with a schoolteacher. Bill stayed and read the newspaper. Bill never read books much but he liked to talk to people who read them.

'Would you like to come to our house for dinner sometimes, Mr Fortlow?' Oscar Minette asked Socrates at the door at closing time.

'Yeah,' he said.

'We're in the Holy Church retirement residence on Forty-seven and Central.'

'I know where it's at.'

'Come over on Sunday, 'bout four. We'll have supper.'

Socrates expected a much larger apartment. People like the Minettes should have had a long dining table with thick carpets and a kitchen big enough to feed an army of grandchildren. But it was just two small rooms and a kitchen that Big Bill wouldn't have fit into. The floor was unfinished wood and the table didn't leave room for a bread basket with the three dinner plates on it. One window only and no bookshelves.

'Everything we ever had is in the Capricorn,' Oscar Minette told Socrates over baked chicken. 'Winnie and I couldn't have children and so we started the store forty-nine years ago. It's always been more spiritual than anything but we keep books for everybody.'

Dinner was only one small chicken but Winifred baked it until the skin was crisp and salty and meat fell from the bone. Socrates found himself more hungry after the meal than he was when he sat down.

But he wasn't complaining.

The Minettes had met James Baldwin and Langston Hughes and both Martin Luther Kings. They hosted plays on the weekends and had gone to Africa with Louis Armstrong in the sixties.

'We don't have any money in the bank,' Winifred said. 'But our lives are like treasure chests.' She looked at her husband and they linked hands across the table.

'I can see it,' Socrates told them. He felt himself relaxing in their home. It was a comfort that he'd given up on years before he went to prison. It made him so happy that he was afraid to talk,

207

afraid that he might say something to break the spell.

'Where's your people from, Mr Fortlow?' Oscar asked. Socrates was sitting on the couch while Winifred sat in her dinner chair, Mr Minette stood because sitting cramped his back.

'Indiana.'

'They still there?'

Socrates waited a moment before saying, 'I guess.'

'You haven't heard from them?' Winifred asked with a big sorry smile on her fine-featured face.

'I was in prison,' Socrates said for the first time that he didn't have to. 'When I went away my family forgot me. All except my mother, but she died soon after I was incarcerated.'

'That's wrong,' Oscar said in a somber tone. 'Wrong.'

'Oh, I don't know,' Socrates replied. He felt so comfortable that he could have fallen off to sleep on that couch. 'I was a bad man, really bad. I don't blame anybody for not wantin' to claim my blood.'

'But you got out,' Winifred said. 'You paid your debt and now you're doing good.'

'I got out okay, but you know I was mean then too. They let me go 'cause all I did was kill black folks. They don't think that black folks are worth a whole life in a white man's jail. But I wasn't cured. I was still mean an' still confused. You know my main problem was that

I was never sure what was right. You know – absolutely sure.'

The Minettes both stared. Socrates was certain that they weren't afraid of him.

'But you did change?' Oscar Minette asked.

'Comin' down to your store. Listenin' to Minty an' Roland an' Stanley Pete; gettin' a ride home from Big Bill now and then. An' watchin' you two just sit back lettin' it all happen. It was like I was seein' through your eyes. I'd let my mind be smilin' an' carin' 'bout people when I knew that they was wrong. Somehow watchin' you made me see myself. You know what I mean?'

'You're a good man, Mr Fortlow.'

'No.'

Later on, after rhubarb pie, Oscar said, 'No, you're wrong, Socrates. You are a good man.'

Winifred had gone to bed. Her good-night handshake was like a handful of icy feathers in a dream.

'Why you say that, Oscar?'

'Because you know, in your heart, that there's something good in the world in spite of all the bad you've seen and been. You come out to the bookshop and talk to those men because you know that there's something good in the world and you want it.'

'What good is this you talkin' 'bout?'

'Purpose, Mr Fortlow. Purpose. We're all here for a reason. There is a divine plan. Good men want to find their place in that plan. That's you.'

'You mean a plan like in the Bible?'

'No, not in a book. Not in a church or temple or mosque.

You see it, don't you? Where did life come from? A rock fell in some mud and then lightning struck? A muddy cell turns into a pollywog and he comes to be a frog; the frog jumps up high until he's a bird and then finally a man falls out of the sky? No, all that's just science fiction.'

Socrates could see that Oscar Minette had given his divine plan lots of thought.

'What there is is a plan, a direction that every living thing is moving toward. There's a high sign but not everybody can see it. But you saw it.' Oscar Minette smiled with deep expectations at his new friend.

There hadn't even been dinner wine at the Minettes' table but Socrates felt drunk. It was late at night and he was seated in the presence of the first man he'd respected since he was a boy in Indiana. Church songs kept coming into Socrates' mind; they played in the back of his head while he tried to keep from nodding to their beats.

There seemed to be music in the room. Music in the way the chairs faced each other, music in the sounds from elsewhere in the building. Socrates wanted to dance for the first time in his fifty years.

'I don't . . .' Socrates said and then stalled. 'I don't . . . really believe it, Mr Minette.'

Mr Minette's smile faded into sad resignation.

'No sir,' Socrates went on. 'I wanna believe you. And I sure don't wanna make you mad. But there ain't no plan. No sir there ain't. There's rules; all kindsa rules. And rules is always made to put money in another man's pocket; food in somebody else's children's mouths.

'Only two reasons I come by Capricorn. One is 'cause I like you an' Mrs Minette. You good people. And the other one is 'cause I wanna know how to break the rules. Because any black man that ever did a thing for hisself broke the rules – he had to because the rules say that a black man cain't have nuthin'.

'That's what I learned in prison. You know I shouldn'ta been up in jail. I murdered and I raped and then I murdered again. A man like me shoulda been hung, gassed, and then electrocuted.

But they didn't kill me because I was the best kinda rule-followin' niggah. I killed my own people an' then let myself get caught. To my own people I was a dog, but the men who made the rules threw me a bone and let me live.

'That was the trick for me. I thought I knew what I was doin' but I was just workin' for the men made the rules. Killin' my own people was just part'a the rules. Makin' myself a jailbird was just what they wanted.' Socrates saw that Mr Minette had stopped listening. He was looking into Socrates' eyes; what he saw was a boat that had busted its rope and was now floating with no captain toward a faraway storm.

But Socrates didn't care that Minette couldn't understand him. He was talking now; he had something to say.

'You an' Winifred broke the rules, Oscar,' Socrates said. 'You started that store, made room for black men and women, and didn't take no collection and didn't tell'em what to think. You had me here to dinner an' opened your heart. That's revolution, brother, rebellion against the rule.

'I don't know who make the bird fly, man. But I do know who make it shit on my head. I love you, Oscar. Because you the one showed me the truth.'

3

Socrates said good night soon after he'd finished talking. He received the older man's leathery handshake and then went down Central toward home. He could feel his heart throbbing in his chest as he remembered all the bad things that had happened to him and then the bad that he had done. It was all laid out before him like a feast. He could pick up a memory, look at it, and then put it down again. He was the master, his legs were his to walk on and the street was his to stride.

Each breath was his and every sight was an image in his own eye.

'Hey you!' a harsh voice called from somewhere to his left. 'I'm talkin' to you.'

'What?' Socrates said. When he turned the policemen were climbing out of their car like soldier ants coming out of a hole.

They each carried a baton.

Socrates wished that his blood would stop pounding; that the angry laugh in his throat would subside.

'Take your hands out of your pockets!' The first rule had been made.

'Where you going?' one cop asked, none too kind.

'I'm just here, officer,' Socrates said. He wanted to giggle but held that down.

The two men flanked him, standing a good four feet away. They could see his strength and his size. They had seen what could happen to policemen who got too close to the fire.

'What the fuck's that s'posed to mean? I asked you a question.'

'Let's see some ID,' the second cop said.

'It's in my pocket,' Socrates apologized.

One of the cops made a motion with his baton as if he was about to strike. But Socrates didn't flinch or dodge, he just stood there waiting for permission, the second rule, to reach into his pocket.

'Don't be a smartass,' a policeman said. 'Take out some ID.'

It was a state registration card for a man who had spent twenty-seven years in prison.

'We got us a jailbird, Simon,' one cop said.

'What you doin' out here at night?'

And then there was a gun pointing at Socrates' eye. He regarded the weapon and said nothing. No *yes sirs*, no *fuck yous*, no *I was just going home, officers*.

While Simon pointed his pistol the other white man went through Socrates' pockets. He found a key to the padlock that secured the ex-convict's front door, a small pocket knife with two razor-sharp blades, four dollars and twenty-eight cents, a folded-up form that gave the receiving hours for the South Central recycling center, and a small bag of salted nuts, half eaten.

Simon was standing closer than he should have. Socrates figured that if he hit Simon first the other cop would be easy to fell. He knew from experience that he could kill a man with one punch.

'I'm goin' home,' Socrates said. There was no apology or rancor in his tone.

'What's the knife for?' Simon asked.

'To cut,' Socrates said, 'anything need cuttin'.'

C-plus, Socrates thought to himself when he returned to his back-alley apartment. In those days he was still sleeping on three area rugs piled one on top of the other. He wrote the grade down on a piece of paper. For years he gave himself a grade every day. Anytime he wrote down *failure* somebody had been hurt by those big rock-breaking hands.

4

The Canyon minimall was burnt black from riot fires. The books were scattered all over the parking lot. The cash register lay shattered on the asphalt. Socrates hadn't been to the store for years. After his talk with Oscar he didn't feel the same welcome. Everyone was still nice but the warmth was gone. He dropped by about once a week for a while, just to say hello.

One day he realized that he hadn't been there in over a year.

There was someone moving around inside, in the back room behind the burnt-out desk. The roof was mostly burned away but pieces of ceiling could still fall; looting a destroyed bookstore seemed like a fool's enterprise.

But Socrates went in to see who it was. If it was a looter he'd get an F that day.

'Roland? Roland, is that you?'

'Who're you?' the small, potbellied, strawberry-brown man said. He was thin and frail, and completely bald.

'It's Socco, Socrates. I met you right here eight years ago.'

'Oh. Oh yeah, yeah. You the one always talkin' 'bout fightin'. You see what it gets ya?'

'What happened, Roland? Where's the Minettes?'

'Winifred been dead three years now.'

'Dead?' The sweet smoke took on the odor of death for Socrates. 'Dead how?'

'Heart attack. She was right behind her counter. Just keeled over. I was there. Not a thing we could do.'

'What about Oscar?' Socrates asked.

'Alanna Hersey called him an' told'im 'bout the store. Hour two later he had a stroke.'

Big Bill had died from a heart attack. Minty had been shot dead and nobody ever knew why. Roland had cancer. He had just finished his chemotherapy when the riots broke out.

'Riots?' Roland said to Socrates. They were having breakfast at a McDonald's outside the ring of fire that was South Central L.A. 'I thought you'd call it a rebellion like these folks out here is doin'.'

'I know why too,' Socrates said. 'It feels like rebellion. Like a prison riot – men fightin' for their freedom. That always feels like a revolution. But you know, you burn down your own home in the face'a the enemy an' it's just followin' his rule; doin' what he want you to. Oscar was a rebel. But burnin' down his sto' was just what the man in blue wants. And you know I feel it too. I wanted to loot and burn. I wanted to firebomb a police car an' then take their guns an' shoot down helicopters. But them helicopters woulda crashed in my own

216

people's homes, an' they woulda killed a hunnert innocent Negroes just to bring me down.'

Roland didn't argue with Socrates. They became friends in his last days.

Socrates brought Roland groceries from Bounty Supermarket once a week and then stayed to read to the dying man from the Bible.

They didn't make it through Genesis.

Socrates wrote a speech for Roland's funeral but because nobody came he never read it. Instead he bought a Bible and took to bringing it up to his grave once a week. He read it out loud, a page at a time.

FIREBUG

1

One Thursday morning Socrates met with Stony Wile while Stony was on his coffee break from Avon Imports.

'Yeah, Folger live out on Winnant Terrace in Compton,' Stony said.

'He still know a lotta cops?' Socrates asked.

'What is this, Socco?'

'What is what? All I wanna know is if Folger know some cops out there in the street.'

'You don't talk to cops, Socco.' Stony was a stocky man, an ex-ship welder with salt-and-pepper hair and gray-brown skin. 'You don't talk to them.'

Stony glanced down the alley. His boss was looking out of the warehouse loading dock toward the two friends.

'Bono always think somebody stealin' if they meet somebody out here,' Stony said.

'Gimme your cousin's address,' Socrates insisted.

'Okay,' Stony said. 'But . . .'

'But what?'

'This ain't gonna be no trouble now is it, Socco?'

'Trouble? What's that s'posed to mean, Stony? You think I'm the kinda man mess wit' folks?'

'I think you're serious, Mr Fortlow. Damn serious. I don't want you goin' out to Folger if you on some kinda campaign.'

'I ain't on nuthin', Stony. I need to know sumpin' an' maybe Folger could help – that's all.'

2

'Forty-two years,' Folger Wile was saying, seated with Socrates Fortlow on his rickety front porch. 'Forty-two years an' they put me out in the street. Don't even let me come back and sit around now and then. Too many rules, too many kids wit' guns an' badges, that's what it is. That's not how a police department should be run.'

He was sixty-seven but looked fifteen years older. Teeth missing, and wrinkled as a plucked bird. Folger's eyes didn't seem to focus on anything in particular.

'You know a good cop I could talk to?' Socrates asked after nearly an hour-long lecture on the faults of the LAPD.

Dispatcher was the only job that Folger ever had. He had fallen apart in his retirement. His lawn was dead and brown, blue paint peeled from the walls of his house.

'You hear 'bout them fires?' Folger asked. 'One of 'em went up last night.'

Everyone had been talking about them. The fires. Abandoned stores, abandoned houses.

'They say that dead man was a squatter,' Folger said, a glimmer of glee in his distracted eyes. 'Woman was his girlfriend. They was playin' house just like they had real jobs and a mortgage.'

The first people killed in a dozen fires set.

'Some people sayin' that it's the fire department doin' arson for the white landlords' insurance policies.' Folger could have talked on forever, all he needed was a warm body with ears to sit by and breathe. 'I think it's the Koreans myself. They wanna own all'a the black folks' homes. You know it's really just what they call a, what they call a peacetime invasion. Koreans gonna be all over here. Korean bosses with Mexican slaves and they won't be no room for no black people at all.'

'I'ont know about all that, Folger. Some'a the Koreans real nice people. It's just them damn businessmen wanna steal everything we got. And businessmen come in all colors – even black.'

Folger sneered at Socrates' weak defense. He wasn't going to be convinced, but Socrates didn't care. He was thinking about Ira Giles. About how Ira had all of his privileges taken away in an Indiana jail. They sentenced him to biscuits and water for sixty days.

On day sixty-one they gave him biscuits and water again – as a joke.

Ira cut his mattress open and shoved an open book of matches inside. He lit a single match and ignited the book. The cot caught and four guards came in to put out the fire. Ira stabbed two of them before they could tell what he was doing. He killed the third one, but number four, Harvey Schott, laid him low.

Socrates had always considered fire as an ally since that day; even though they executed Ira. He'd ordered biscuits and water for his last meal.

'You're wrong, Mr Fortlow.'

'Say what, Folger?'

'It's gotta be some kinda conspiracy. Look at me. Look. I worked hard my whole life an' now I ain't got a thing. I got eight hunnert dollars in retirement comin' in and a thousand dollars worf'a bills. You cain't tell me that's a couple'a slumlords doin'. Noooo, no. That shit go all the way to the top. The top. You see that, don't ya?'

'Maybe it go to the heart, Mr Wile,' Socrates said.

'Say what?'

'Maybe just the whole thing is rotten. Us, them, the other guy too. Maybe somethin' spoiled was thrown in with the bunch of us a long time ago and now the only way to settle it is to burn it all down, all of it. Like them houses.'

Folger looked closely at Socrates while rubbing his hand up and down the left side of his face.

'I got to take my nap soon,' he said.

'All right then,' Socrates replied. 'But tell me,

do you know a cop I could talk to? A black man knows he's black?'

3

Socrates spent the afternoon boxing groceries and making deliveries around West Los Angeles and Beverly Hills. It was summer and hot outside but Bounty Supermarket ran from cool at the checkout registers to cold over by the freezer aisles.

Socrates was the oldest employee of the store. His surly appearance and incredible strength delighted the young black girls who worked the electric-eye cash registers. And for some reason the older white ladies preferred him to the younger men to deliver their packages.

Socrates worked extra hard that day, unloading a big shipment of canned goods from General Foods. He threw out double boxes so fast that the young men had a hard time keeping up.

'Hey, Socco,' Bruce Tynan whined. 'Slow down.' The other boys had slipped away on break and never returned.

The Beverly Hills teenager was a football star at high school. He was a good kid, even though he was white, and Socrates liked him.

Dr Tynan, a rich surgeon who owned his own hospital, didn't want his son working in the store but Bruce wanted to earn his money and defied his old man.

'Okay, quarterback, I'll give ya a rest.' Socrates climbed out of the delivery truck and sat on a stack of boxes. He smiled when he saw that Bruce was trying to hide his heavy breathing.

Socrates waited for a while, until Bruce had caught his breath.

'Hey, Bruce?'

'Yeah, Socco?'

'What would you do if you knew, or you thought you knew, that a man had killed two people?'

Bruce's face flushed, and his eyes looked away, toward the delivery door.

'Huh?' he grunted.

'You heard me.'

'I'd go to the police. I'd tell.'

'But what if,' Socrates asked, 'what if it wasn't on purpose?'

'Then they'd find him innocent in court.'

'Naw. It was a mistake but he was doin' somethin' wrong. They'd still fry his ass.'

Socrates watched the doctor's son trying to keep up with the problem.

'Would he do it again?' Bruce asked at last.

'What?'

'Whatever he did that got those people killed?'

Socrates stood up and hefted two boxes of fruit cocktail in his arms.

'I'ont know. It was just some magazine article I read,' Socrates said. 'Come on. Let's move some boxes.'

4

Denther's Bar and Grill was a cop café on Normandie. It had wood frame windows, old-time metal venetian blinds, and a cursive neon sign that said Café in blue and Open in red. Only cops, and the women who desired them, went to Denther's. You could smoke in there, kick back and relax. Anything you said was among cops, safe.

Nobody robbed Denther's. Nobody worried about building codes or closing hours – or drugs, or sex.

They had a jukebox that was free and three young waitresses who wore hot pants and thigh-high patent-leather boots. Among the waitresses there was a white girl, a black one, and a Latina.

Denther's was a cop paradise, or so Folger claimed.

Socrates entered the door at nine-thirty exactly. He was still wearing his Bounty blue-and-green T-shirt but that wasn't enough to fool those cops.

The jukebox was playing disco but the conversation nearly stopped. Socrates waded through the dense crowd of men. A couple resisted his advance but Socrates was a strong man, he bulled his way through, cautiously, not pushing hard enough to start a row.

At the bar he asked, 'Kenneth Shreve in here?'

The bartender, a small man, didn't answer.

Socrates asked his question again.

'What do you want?' a white man seated at the bar asked Socrates.

'I want Kenneth Shreve.'

'What for?'

'You his mother?' Socrates asked, almost pleasantly.

'You better watch it . . .' The unspoken word dangled at the end of the white man's sentence. It was an integrated bar. Black cops and white ones patronized Denther's. You couldn't call a man a nigger unless you were a nigger yourself.

The white man didn't use the word but he would have liked to use his fists.

Socrates wondered why he didn't feel afraid.

'You know where I can find Kenneth Shreve?'

'I'm Shreve,' a tall black man said. He had come up behind Socrates.

Socrates turned around. 'Folger Wile sent me.'

Kenneth Shreve was wide as well as tall. His shoulders could have borne Socrates' hefty two hundred and sixty-two pounds. His hands were small but so, Socrates remembered, were Joe Louis's hands.

'What's that old fool want?' Kenneth asked. He could see the long history of felony trailing in Socrates' shadow but he didn't care.

'He want them to extend retirement age at the dispatcher's so that he could have somethin' to do,' Socrates said.

That got a laugh out of Shreve.

225

'Come on,' the cop said. 'Let's sit over at that booth.'

The booth had three black cops and two black women crammed on the bench. One woman had a hand in the lap of the man on either side of her. She was looking back and forth at them – wide-eyed. The men were looking into each other's eyes.

All that broke up when Sergeant Shreve came by. He didn't even say anything. He just walked up and the men hustled the women out of the stall.

'Hey,' one of the young women said. 'What's wrong?'

They sat and the quiet bartender brought beers. Socrates downed his with one swallow.

'What's your name?'

'Socrates Fortlow.' The ex-convict's jaw clamped shut after his name. He wanted to start talking but he found that he couldn't.

'Well?' Shreve asked. 'What's Shorty want?'

'Excuse me?'

'Shorty. That's what we called Folger.'

'Oh.'

Socrates looked up into the crowded, smoky den. Shreve anticipated him and waved for another beer.

'I got things to do, man. So if you got somethin' for me from Shorty lets hear it.'

Socrates looked at Shreve until the beer came. The big cop wanted to move but he didn't. Socrates thought that the policeman knew somehow that the most important thing in that room was what Socrates had to say.

'I been up in prison,' Socrates said after downing the second brew.

'What for?' the sergeant asked. His face had gone blank. His eyes were all over Socrates.

'Homicide.'

Shreve gave a slight nod to show that he'd already known the answer.

'What you got to do wit' Folger?'

'I'ont even hardly know the man. I know his cousin.'

'And what you want with me?'

'I don't want ya,' Socrates said. 'Shit, man. I'm a jailbird. You know I was made in a prison cell. I don't talk to cops.'

An evil grin formed on Shreve's face. He was a dark brown man with little scars and nicks on his forehead, neck, and jaw. 'Don't fuck with me, Negro,' he said.

'I'm just sayin' that I'm not used to talkin' to cops. It's not easy bein' in this here room.'

'This is the only place you're gonna see me,' Shreve said. 'Unless you wanna go back down to a jail cell.'

'That don't scare me,' Socrates said. 'Ain't nuthin' could happen to me that ain't already happened. Nuthin'.'

'What do you want, man?'

'Back in the joint, man didn't talk to no screw.

They find you doin' that and there was a knife for you.'

'You want to tell me something, but you're scared?' Shreve asked.

'I'm way past scared,' Socrates said. 'Way past that. I'm the one enforce the rules, an' I ain't never broke it.'

'But you gonna break it now?' Shreve waved for two beers this time.

'Sometimes,' Socrates said. 'you might get to know a guard an' he ain't so bad. I mean, he could be there for you, you know what I mean?'

The beers came and Shreve pushed them both in front of the ex-con. Socrates emptied both of them in less than a minute.

'You want something?' Shreve asked.

'Yeah.' There was a pleasant blank feeling at the back of Socrates' head. It really wasn't enough beer to get him high but he'd forgotten to eat that day.

'I don't want your money, man,' Socrates said. 'I don't want that. What I want is you.'

'Say what?'

5

'A man is innocent until he's proven guilty,' Socrates quoted. 'Do you believe that?'

'If a man did a crime then he's guilty,' Shreve said. He took a deep breath and looked over each shoulder. 'If he didn't he's innocent. That's what I believe.'

'But the law says that a man is innocent unless he is judged otherwise by a panel of his peers. I learnt that up in jail.

'Everybody was guilty up there; didn't matter if they'd done the crime or not. They were guilty because they were found guilty by a panel of their peers.'

'Hey, Kenny.' A drunken black man had staggered up to the booth. He was supported by a young woman under each arm. One of the had a blouse cut so low that Socrates could make out the tops of her nipples. When she saw Socrates looking she smiled and angled her body for him to see better.

'Kenny,' the drunken man said again. 'Let's go on upstairs.' The man cocked the top of his head toward the back door and winked.

Shreve glanced at the door and then at the low-cut girl.

'You go on,' he said. 'I'll be up in a little while.'

'Ooooh,' the women complained in unison.

As they were leaving Shreve said, 'You better cut out this shit and tell me what you got to say, brother.'

'I was just sayin' did you believe that a man is innocent . . .'

'What man?' Shreve asked. 'What man? What the fuck are you talking about?'

Socrates' jaw snapped shut. His teeth ached from the pressure.

'Come on, Fortlow. Talk to me.'

'Fire,' Socrates whispered.

'Say what?'

'Fires. Fires.'

Shreve froze like a stalking cat.

'Them fires,' Socrates said and then the bottom fell out of his diaphragm sucking all his words back down with it.

'The fires in Watts?'

He could still nod.

'You know who's doin' 'em?'

'I don't know nuthin' for sure. Man's innocent, innocent.'

Shreve sat back and rubbed his scarred face.

'It's the reward, right?'

'What reward?'

'Come on, brother. You cain't pull that shit on me. They announced it this morning; fifteen thousand dollars for information leading to the arrest of . . .'

Socrates was up and out of his chair before Shreve could finish his sentence. He was moving fast toward the door; no *excuse mes*, no being careful as he pushed people out of the way.

Outside he walked quickly down the street.

'Uh-uh,' Socrates Fortlow kept saying to himself. 'No, no. They not gonna catch me with that.'

'Fortlow!'

'Uh-uh. Uh-uh, no.'

'Fortlow! Halt!'

The command took over the convict side of Socrates' brain, bringing his legs to a full stop.

'What's wrong with you, man?' Sergeant Shreve said as he caught up with Socrates. He was breathing heavily. 'I've been calling you for three blocks.'

Socrates just shook his head in stubborn denial.

'What's wrong?' Shreve asked again.

'No,' said Socrates as if that answered any question Shreve could ask.

The street downtown was empty, except for a line of homeless men and women reclining against a wall across the street. The traffic lights kept changing color but there was no traffic to heed them.

'No what? Do you know who the South Central firebug is?'

'You cain't buy me, man,' Socrates said. 'I ain't your slave.'

'I don't want the money, Fortlow. You could have it. All I want is the man. He's out there killing people. That's why you came here, right? You don't want to turn in a man 'cause you're an excon but you still don't want people to die.'

The flames in Socrates' mind seemed to flare on that dark street. Ira Giles swinging his homemade knife while his flames were crawling right up his back. *Screamin' devil right outta hell*, somebody had said. They all laughed and spat and said that the guards should have known better than to give Ira biscuits and water for an extra day. It was their own fault. You can push a man only so far and then you've got to let up – or kill him.

'Let's go down to the station, Fortlow. Let's make a report.'

'Wait up,' Socrates said. 'Wait up.'

'What?'

'He's innocent right?'

'If he is then why are you talking to me?'

'I want him treated like a man, officer. I want you,' Socrates jabbed his finger into Shreve's chest, 'to tell me that you gonna go down there and make sure that he's treated like a man. I don't want him beat, or cursed, or cheated. Folger told me that you do a fair deal with Negroes and whites too. I want a fair deal for the man I give you or so help me God I'll be out there in the streets burnin' just like he done.'

Shreve put a hand on his bruised chest.

'I'll be there, you can bet on that. And he'll get as fair a deal as I can give.'

6

Socrates told Sergeant Shreve his story at the downtown police station after signing a document that stated he was giving evidence about the South Central firebug.

There wasn't much to say.

Socrates had seen Ira Giles through his cell grate after Ira had stabbed those men. He'd been beaten and stomped. His right arm was raw from fire. But Ira was grinning. His face was slick with sweat and his eyes were big enough to scare a wild animal from its den. He was gibbering and laughing; he would have danced if the guards hadn't kept punching him and making him walk straight ahead.

Socrates had been out walking on the night of the last fire, the fatal one. He heard the fire engines and smelled the smoke. The over-weight Negro who capered toward Socrates didn't even see the ex-con. He was at his own little party. His chunky legs switched in their work pants.

'It was the smell at first,' Socrates told Shreve. 'Then it was the way he was sayin' words that didn't make no sense. He was sweatin' heavy too but it was the dancin', it was the dancin' made me follow him home.'

'That's all?' said Andrew Collins, Shreve's patrol partner. 'That's what you got us down here for?'

Socrates told them how he waited for Ponzelle Richmond to leave his house again.

'I looked in the windah an' seen gasoline cans with a lotta bottles an' rags around,' he said.

He didn't tell them how he pried the lock off the back door. He didn't tell them about the diary.

233

'Let's check it out, Andy.' Shreve said to his shaggy white partner. 'We'll get back to you, Mr Fortlow.'

7

'I tried to talk to'em,' Socrates was telling Stony Wile after it was all over. 'I thought that maybe I could make a difference. You know if I said I wouldn't cooperate unless they promised to play fair?'

'They played it fair, Socco,' Stony said. They were sitting in Socrates' house on a Monday afternoon, each drinking from his own bottle of Cold Duck. Stony had been laid off from Avon Imports. 'How could they help it if the man sees 'em comin' an' shoots hisself? You cain't blame the cops for ev'rything.'

Socrates took another drink from his bottle. He wanted to hit Stony but held back.

They drank for a long time after that.

And then they drank some more.

'Socco?'

'Yeah, Stony?'

'What about that money?'

'What money?'

'The reward. I know they keep them Crime Watchers names quiet but if you turnt Ponzelle in then you musta got somethin'.'

'Cops kept the reward 'cept for a few hunnert

dollars,' Socrates said. 'I spent the first hunnert on the liquor you helpin' me drink.'

Socrates lit a match and took a hundred dollar bill from his pocket. He set fire to the corner of the bill.

'Want it?' he asked Stony.

Stony grabbed for the bill from Socrates' hand and snubbed out the flame with his thick workman's fingers.

'What's wrong wit' you? This here's a hundred dollars.'

'And it's yours, Stony. That's your share for helpin' t'kill Ponzelle. All you had to do was grab for it.'

8

Socrates awoke in the night thinking about the hundred and forty-seven hundred dollar bills that were buried in his meager yard. Three feet down they rested in their plastic bag. And with them the diary of the firebug.

The cops had found maps, clippings, notes, and paraphernalia enough to convince them that Ponzelle was their man. But Socrates had the diary.

He remembered one part by heart:

. . . if I could just get them to see that we got to burn down all this mess we done stacked up and

hacked up and shacked up all around us. If they could see the torch of change, the burning of flames all around their eyes. We could come together in fire and steel and blood and love and make ourselves a home. Not this shit, not this TV and church world. Not this jungle of dirty clothes and Christmas seals. Not ham on Sunday and grandma's dead already and can't even eat her piece . . .

BLACK DOG

1

'How does your client plead, Ms Marsh?' the pencil-faced judge asked. He was wearing a dark sports jacket that was a size or two too big for his bony frame.

'Not guilty, your honor,' the young black lawyer said, gesturing with her fingers pressed tightly together and using equally her lips, tongue, and teeth.

'Fine.' The judge had been distracted by something on his desk. 'Bail will be . . .'

'Your honor,' spoke up the prosecutor, a chubby man who was the color of a cup of coffee with too much milk mixed in. 'Before you decide on bail the people would like to have it pointed out that Mr Fortlow is a convincted felon. He was found guilty of a double homicide in Indiana in nineteen sixty and was sentenced to life in that state; he spent almost thirty years in prison.'

'Twenty-seven years, your honor,' Brenda Marsh articulated.

So much respect, so much honor, Socrates

Fortlow thought. A harsh laugh escaped his lips.

'And,' Brenda Marsh continued. 'He's been leading a respectable life here in Los Angeles for the past eight years. He's employed full-time by Bounty Supermarket and he hasn't had any other negative involvement with the law.'

'Still, your honor,' the bulbous Negro said, 'Mr Fortlow is being tried for a violent crime—'

'But he hasn't been convicted,' said Ms Marsh.

'Regardless,' said the nameless prosecutor.

'Your honor . . .'

The Honorable Felix Fisk tore his eyes away from whatever had been distracting him. Socrates thought it was probably a picture magazine; probably about yachting, Socrates thought. He knew, from his days in prison, that many judges got rich off of the blood of felons.

'All right,' Judge Fisk said. 'All right. Let's see.'

He fumbled around with some papers and produced a pair of glasses from the top of his head. He peered closely at whatever was written and then regarded the bulky ex-con.

'My, my,' the judge muttered.

Socrates felt hair growing in his windpipe.

'The people would like to see Mr Fortlow held without bail, your honor,' chubby said.

'Your honor.' Ms Marsh's pleading didn't seem to fit with her overly precise enunciation. 'Eight years and there was no serious injury.'

'Intent,' the prosecutor said, 'informs the law.'

'Twenty-five thousand dollars bail,' the judge intoned.

A short brown guard next to Socrates grabbed the prisoner's beefy biceps and said, 'Come on.'

Socrates turned around and saw Dolly Straight at the back of the small courtroom. She had red hair and freckles, and a look of shock on her face. When her eyes caught Socrates' gaze she smiled and waved.

Then she ran out of the courtroom while still holding her hand high in greeting.

2

The night before there had been no room in the West L.A. jail so they put Socrates in a secured office for lockup. But now he was at the main courthouse. They took him to a cellblock in the basement crammed with more than a dozen prisoners. Most of them were tattooed; one had scars so violent that he could have been arrested and jailed simply because of how terrible he appeared.

Mostly young men; mostly black and Latino. There were a couple of whites by themselves in a corner at the back of the cell. Socrates wondered what those white men had done to be put in jeopardy like that.

'Hey, brother,' a bearded man with an empty eye socket said to Socrates.

Socrates nodded.

239

'Hey, niggah,' said a big, black, baby-faced man who stood next to the bearded one. 'Cain't you talk?'

Socrates didn't say anything. He went past the men toward an empty spot on a bench next to a stone-faced Mexican.

'Niggah!' the baby face said again.

He laid a hand, not gently, on Socrates' shoulder. But Babyface hesitated. He felt, Socrates knew, the strength in that old shoulder. And in that brief moment Socrates shot out his left hand to grab the young man's throat. The man threw a fist but Socrates caught that with his right hand while increasing the pressure in his left.

The boy's eyes bulged and he went down on his knees as Socrates stood up. First Babyface tried to dislodge the big fist from his throat, then he tried slugging Socrates' arm and side.

While he was dying the men stood around.

Sounds like the snapping of brittle twigs came from the boy's throat.

His dying eyes flitted from one prisoner to another but no one moved to help him.

A few seconds before the boy would have lost consciousness, no more than fifteen seconds before he'd've died, Socrates let go.

The boy sucked in a breath of life so deep and so hoarse that a guard came down to see what was happening.

Some of the men were laughing.

'What's goin' on?' the guard asked.

'I was just showin' the boy a trick,' the big bearded Negro with one eye said.

The guard regarded the boy.

'You okay, Peters?'

There was no voice in Peters's throat but he nodded.

'Okay,' the guard said. 'Now cut it out down here.'

Socrates took his place on the bench. The fight was just an initiation. Now everyone in the cell knew: Socrates was not a man to be taken lightly.

'Fortlow?' the same guard called out forty-five minutes later.

'Yo.'

'Socrates Fortlow?'

'That's right.' It hadn't been long but the feeling of freedom had already drained from Socrates' bones and flesh.

He'd checked out every man in the holding cell; witnessed one of the white men get beaten while his buddy backed away. He'd made up his mind to go against the bearded Negro, Benny Hite, if they remained in the cell together.

Benny was a leader and naturally wanted to hold everyone else down. But Socrates wouldn't go down for anyone and so there had to be blood before there could be sleep.

'Come with me,' the guard said. He had two large policemen with him.

3

'Hi, Mr Fortlow,' Dolly Straight said. Her skin was pale under thousands of orange and brown freckles. 'I posted your bail.'

They'd given him his street clothes back but it was too late; the body lice, crabs, from the prison garb had already begun to make him itch.

'What you doin'?' he asked the young woman in front of the courthouse.

'I'm parked illegally up the block,' she said, hurrying down the concrete stairs. 'I didn't know it would take so long to give them the money and get you out.'

Socrates tried to ask again, *why*, but Dolly kept running ahead of him.

'I hope they haven't towed it,' she said.

Her pickup was from the fifties, a Dodge. It was sky-blue with a flatbed back that had an animal cage moored in the center.

'Come on,' she said, taking the parking ticket from under the windshield wiper. 'Get in.'

'What's this all about?' Socrates asked as they made their way from downtown.

'I put up your bail.' Dolly was redheaded, plain-faced, and she had green eyes that blazed. There were fans of tiny wrinkles around her eyes but she was no more than forty.

'What for?'

'Because of Bruno,' she said as if it should have been obvious.

'Who's that?'

'The dog. That's what I called him. I mean you can't take care of somebody if he doesn't even have a name. Most of your best vets always name their patients if they don't get a name from the owners.'

'Oh,' Socrates said. He was wondering what to do with his liberation. Some men who'd spent as many years behind bars as Socrates had wanted to go back to jail; they liked the order that they found there.

'I'd rather be dead,' he said.

'Excuse me?'

'Why'd you get me outta there?'

'Because,' Dolly said. 'Because I know what you did you did because of Bruno. He was almost dead when you brought him in to me. And when those policemen came to arrest you I just got mad. They think that they can just walk in anywhere.'

He hadn't been looking for a fight. It was an early work day because he'd had to help with inventory at the supermarket and that started at four in the morning. He'd worked twelve hours and was tired. A dog, big and black, was nosing around, begging for food and Socrates told him to *git*. The dog got himself into the street and a speeding Nissan slammed him down. The man didn't even hit the brakes until after the accident.

Socrates was already to the dog when the white

243

man backed up and parked. The poor dog was scrabbling with his front paws, trying to rise, and whining from the pain in his crushed hind legs.

Socrates just wanted to help. As far as he was concerned the white man broke his own nose.

'How you know why I did what I did?' Socrates asked Dolly.

'Because I went back to where you told me the accident happened. I wanted to find out if the owner was somewhere nearby. I thought that I'd have to put Bruno to sleep but I didn't want to do that until I talked to the owner.

'But there wasn't an owner. Bruno didn't have a home but I met an old lady who saw what happened. That's what I told your lawyer. You know I don't know if Miss Marsh would have gone down there or not. But I told her about Bruno and Mrs Galesky and then she told me how I could put up your bail.

'I don't know if I'd want her for a lawyer, Mr Fortlow.'

'Why's that?'

'She was trying to tell me how you were a convicted felon and that this charge against you was tough and you might run if you could. Even after I told her that I knew that you were innocent. I thought you black people helped each other out?'

'Dog gonna live?' Socrates asked.

Dolly's face got harder and Socrates found himself liking her in spite of her youth and race.

'I don't know,' she said. 'His legs are broken

244

and so's his hip. I don't even think they could do a replacement on a human hip that was that bad. His organs seem fine. No bleeding inside but he'll never use those legs again.'

They drove on toward Dolly's Animal Clinic on Robertson near Olympic.

4

Bruno was a biggish dog, sixty pounds or more, and little of that was fat. He was unconscious in a big cage on an examining table in Dolly's clinic.

'I gave him a tranc,' she said. 'I don't like to do that but he was in so much pain and his crying bothered my other patients.'

In a large room connected to the examining room Socrates could see rows of cages that ran from small to large. Most of the 'patients' were dogs and cats fitted with casts or bandages or attached to odd machines. But there was also a monkey, three different kinds of birds, a goat, and something that looked like a tiny albino sloth.

'Would he die if you left him alone?' Socrates asked. It was ten o'clock or later. There was only him and Dolly in the small animal clinic. He realized that he was pinching the skin through his pants pockets and stopped.

'I don't know,' Dolly said. 'I don't think so. His vitals are strong. You'd have to get his bones set as well as possible and then keep him immobile for a couple of weeks. All that and he'd live. But he'd have to crawl.'

'Anything's better than prison or death.'

'You pick that up in the jail?' Dolly asked.

Socrates realized that he was scratching again.

'My dad used to get that all the time,' she said. 'He was a political activist down San Diego in the sixties. I remember they'd bust up his protests and beat him until he had black blood coming out. But the only thing he ever complained about was getting crabs in jail. He used to say that they could at least keep it clean in there.' She smiled a very plain smile and said, 'I got some soap'll clear that up in two days.'

Bruno whimpered in his cage.

'I'ma be in a cage if they put me down for assault,' he said.

'But I gave your lawyer Mrs Galesky's number. I'm sure she'll straighten it out.'

'You are, huh?'

'Yeah.' Dolly's homely smile was growing on him. 'I got a house right in back here,' she said. 'You could stay in the guest bed.'

5

Dolly heated apple cider spiced with cinnamon sticks. Then she made sandwiches out of alfalfa sprouts, grilled chicken, gruyère cheese, and avocado. Socrates had four sandwiches and over a quart of cider.

Who knew when he'd be eating again?

Dolly had fed, petted, and talked to each patient and then led Socrates out of the back door of the clinic. There was a yard in back and a large flowering tree that was dark and sweet-smelling. Past the tree was a wooden fence. The gate in the fence opened to a beautiful little house.

'Nobody can ever see my house if I don't invite them,' Dolly said to Socrates as she fumbled around for her keys. 'I like that.'

'Where's your father?' Socrates asked after supper. It was late, past midnight, and Dolly was folding out the bed in the living room.

'He died,' she said. 'He was always big and strong but then he just got old one year and passed away.'

'Didn't he ever tell you about people like me?'

'He never knew anybody like you, Mr Fortlow.'

'How the hell you know what I'm like?' Socrates said belligerently. 'Didn't you hear what they said about me in that courtroom?'

Dolly looked up.

With a stern gaze she said, 'I know what you're thinking. You're thinking why would she take a man, a convicted murderer, and take him back here in her house? A man like that could rob me, rape me, kill me.' Then her serious face turned into a smile. 'But I don't have a choice so I can't be worried about it.'

'What you mean you ain't got no choice?'

'Because my father died when I was only twelve and my mother just left,' she said. 'Because the only one who ever loved me was my dog, Buster. And the only thing I ever knew was how to love him and to take care of him. If I see anyone who cares about animals they're okay with me. I treat them like human beings.'

'So you mean that anybody bring a hurt animal to you can sit at your table and sleep in your guest bed?'

'No,' Dolly said. She was hurt.

'Then what do you mean?'

'I mean that a dog is a living being just like you'n me. It doesn't matter if there is a God or not. Life is what's important. You're not like one of those rich bitches that shave a dog like he was some kind of fuckin' hedge and then bring him to me so I could castrate him.

'You knocked a man down and then carried that big dog over a mile. You went to jail because that dog has a right. How can I look at that and not do all I can do for you?'

6

Socrates was up late in his foldout bed. It was an old couch and the bed was more comfortable than

248

his own. There was no sound coming through the walls in the house. There was a sweet odor. For a long time Socrates let his mind wander trying to figure out the smell. It was familiar but he couldn't place it.

Finally he realized that the scent was from the tree outside. A window must have been open. It was the thought of an open window that got Socrates to giggle uncontrollably. He hadn't slept next to an open window in over forty years.

7

Over the next three weeks Socrates dropped by Dolly's every day after work. He talked to Bruno and accepted meals in the back house.

'If Bruno live an' I don't go to jail,' he promised Dolly, 'I'll take him home wit' me and keep'im for my pet.'

The trial came four weeks after that declaration.

8

'You're with the Public Defender's Office?' the judge, Katherine Hemp, asked Brenda Marsh.

'Yes, your honor,' Brenda replied. 'I've just been with them three months now.'

'And how does your client plead, Ms Marsh?'

asked Judge Hemp, an older woman with gray hair and sad eyes.

'Not guilty, your honor.'

'I don't want to drag this thing out, counselor. I have a full caseload and all we want to know here is if your client assaulted, um,' the judge looked down at her notes, 'Benheim Lunge.'

'I appreciate the court's time, Judge Hemp. I have only three witnesses and each of them has less than forty-five minutes of testimony.' Brenda Marsh spoke in her own fashion, as usual, pronouncing each word separately as if it had come in its own individual wrapper. Socrates wondered if Brenda thought that she sounded like a white woman talking like that.

'Benheim Lunge,' said the tall young man in the witness seat. He might have been handsome if it wasn't for the sour twist of his lips.

'. . . and were you then assaulted by this man?' asked Conrad MacAlister, the pudgy café-au-lait prosecutor.

'Yes sir. He hit me. I'm in good shape but he must've been boxing in that prison or something.'

Socrates' eyes wandered over to the jurors' box. They were mostly women and he could see that they were appalled by Lunge's description of his broken nose and whiplash from just one swipe of the ex-convict's fist.

'Thank you, Mr Lunge.' MacAlister smiled at Brenda Marsh. 'Your witness.'

Brenda Marsh got up purposefully and stalked over to Lunge. 'Did you, Mr Lunge, go up to where the dog lay with a brick in your hand?'

'No.'

'I see. Tell me, Mr Lunge, what is your profession?'

'I sell sporting goods. My father owns a store on Rodeo Drive and I run it.'

'So,' asked Brenda. 'Then you don't have a medical background?'

'No.'

'But didn't you tell Mr Fortlow that the dog was done for and that he should be put out of his suffering? And don't you think it was likely that the defendent thought that you intended to kill the dog with the brick you held?'

'Objection,' said Prosecutor MacAlister. 'Mr Lunge has already stated that he didn't have a brick in his hand.'

'A stone then?' asked Ms Marsh. 'Did you have a stone, Mr Lunge?'

'No.'

'Did you have anything in your hands when you approached the wounded dog and Mr Fortlow on Olympic Boulevard?'

'Um, well, I don't remember. I, uh, I might have grabbed a, a, a, you know, a thing, a ten-pound weight I keep in the backseat.'

'A ten-pound weight? What was this weight made from?'

'Iron.'

'So, you approached Mr Fortlow with ten pounds of iron in your hand?'

'How was I to know what would happen? For all I knew it was his dog. I wanted to help but I wanted to protect myself too. He looked, well, dangerous. And he was big. I knew I had to stop for hitting the dog but I wanted to protect myself too.'

'And did you say that you'd kill the dog with the weight? Didn't you say that you wanted to stop his pain?'

'Absolutely not. I mean I never said that I wanted to kill the dog. I thought he was going to die, though, I mean you should have seen him. He was a mess.'

9

'That man right there,' said Marjorie Galesky. She was pointing at Benheim Lunge. Dolly Straight had already testified that Socrates Fortlow came to her clinic with the bleeding and crying black dog in his arms. He'd carried the sixty-two-pound dog eleven blocks to get him care.

'. . . I was sitting in my front yard,' seventy-nine-year-old Mrs Galesky said, 'like always when it's over seventy-two degrees. It was getting cooler and I was about to go in when I see this car run over that poor dog. It hit him and then the tires ran over his legs. This man,' she said, pointing at Socrates, 'the black one, had gone up to help the dog when the other man, the one driving the car, comes running over with a brick in his hand. At least it looked like a brick. They say it was a weight, whatever that means, but it was big and that man came running over with it. He said something to the black man and then he tried to get at the dog. First off the black man pushed the white one and then he hauled off and hit him.' The old woman was a few inches under five feet and slight. She looked like an excited child up there on the stand. There was an ancient glee at the memory of the punch. Socrates tried to keep from smiling.

10

'Socrates Fortlow,' he answered when asked to identify himself. 'Yes I did,' he said when asked if he struck Benheim Lunge. 'He hit the dog and drove off for all I knew. I went up and was tryin' to see what I could do when he come up with a chunk'a metal in his hand. He was lookin' all over an' said that it'd be better to put the dog outta his misery. Then he said that he wanted to take the dog in his car. I said I'd go along but he told me that there wasn't room for me an' the dog too. I told him that I'd seen a animal hospital not far and that I'd carry the dog there. He said no. Then I said no. He went for the dog an' he still had the iron in his hand. I put up my hand to stop'im but he just kept comin'. So I hit him once. You know I didn't

253

mean to do all that to him but he wasn't gonna take that dog. Uh-uh.'

11

'We find the defendant guilty of assault,' the foreman of the jury, a black woman, said. She seemed sorry but that was the decision and she stood with it.

12

While waiting for his sentence Socrates would go to visit Bruno every day. Dolly had made a leash with a basket woven from leather straps to hold Bruno up from behind. If Socrates could heft the dog's backside Bruno found that he could propel himself forward by walking with his front legs.

'You could put a clothesline up around your yard, Mr Fortlow,' Dolly said. 'And then attach his basket to it with a pulley. That way he could walk around without you having to help him all the time.'

'Yeah,' Socrates answered. 'Dolly, what you put up behind the ten percent for my bail?'

'The house,' she said.

'Uh-huh.'

Bruno was leaping from one paw to the other, yelping a little now and then because his hip still hurt, and licking the hands of the two new friends.

'If you run I don't care,' Dolly said. 'But you have to take Bruno with you.'

13

Before the sentencing Brenda Marsh had a long meeting with Socrates. He cursed her and pounded his fist down on the table in the little room that the court let them use.

He refused to do what she asked of him.

'You wanna take ev'rything from me?' he asked her.

'I'm trying to keep you out of jail,' she said in her annoying way. 'Do you want to go to jail?'

'There's a lotta things I don't want. One of 'em is that I don't get down on my knees to no man, woman, or child.'

Brenda Marsh did not respond. It was then that Socrates realized that she was probably a very good lawyer.

14

Three days later, after the celebration for Socrates' suspended sentence at Iula's diner, Socrates went to his house with Right Burke, the maimed WWII veteran. They sat in Socrates' poor kitchen while

Bruno lay on the floor laughing and licking the air.

'I hate it, Right. I hate it.'

'You free, ain't ya?'

'Yeah, but I wake up mad as shit every day.'

Brenda Marsh had set up a private meeting with Judge Hemp. She'd pleaded for Socrates' freedom. But the judge said that he'd been found guilty and what could she do?

That's when Brenda revealed her plan for Socrates to apologize to the court, to Benheim Lunge, and to the community. He'd promise to write a letter to be posted on the bus stop where he'd assaulted Benheim and to go to Benheim and ask his pardon. He'd make himself available to the juvenile court to talk to young black children and tell them how he had gone wrong but that he wouldn't do it again.

He'd do an extra fifty hours of community service and for that they could suspend his sentence.

'But you free, Socco. Free, man,' said Right, his best friend. 'That gal did you a favor. 'Cause you know she musta begged that judge. You know after that big trial they just had the court wanna put ev'ry black man they can in the can. Shit. Guilty? Go *straight* to jail!'

'But you know it's just 'cause'a the dog, Right. It's just 'cause'a the dog I said yeah.'

'How's that?'

'He needs me out here. Him and Darryl and you

too, brother. I ain't gonna help nobody in that jail cell or on the run. You know I woulda let them take that white girl's house if it wasn't that I had obligations.'

The dog barked suddenly and put his nose out to be scratched.

'You just a lucky fool, Socrates Fortlow,' Right said.

'You got that right, man. I'm a fool to be who I am and I'm lucky I made it this far. Me an' this black dog here. Shit. Me an' this black dog.'

LAST RITES

1

'I can't do that, Right,' Socrates said. 'I mean I want to but I just cain't bring you a pistol in here. Not wit' you here in Luvia's house and all.'

'I could come to your place,' Right rasped.

He'd been laid up in bed writhing from painful prostate cancer for six weeks. He was too weak to take the bus down to the clinic anymore and too poor to get any doctor to come to him.

'How's that gonna work?' Socrates asked. 'You come into my house an' shoot yourself in the head. Then I go to the police an' say that I thought it was just a toy an' you was just jokin'?'

'I could take it to the park.' Right Burke winced at a pain somewhere below his stomach. He waved his gnarled and useless hand to shoo the agony from the room.

'Man, you could hardly make it half a block last time we walked.'

'Then I'll walk down the block, goddammit!' Tears spurted out of Right's eyes. 'I shouldn't

258

never'a listened to Luvia. I shouldn'ta ever'a give up my piece.'

Socrates grabbed his friend's paralyzed hand and held tight. He sat there for over an hour, until Right slipped off into a doze. Luvia Prine, tall, brown, and skeletal herself, had looked in now and then. Socrates found her in the hall when he left his sleeping, dying friend.

He reached into his pocket and came out with a thin fold of five bills. 'Here's fi'e hunnert dollars, Vi,' he said. 'You get Hiram's ambulette and go down to that clinic with'im. Get that doctor to do some straight talk. You can keep whatever's left over for whatever else he need.'

'Where'd this money come from, Socrates Fortlow?' Luvia asked without taking her hands from her apron pocket.

'You would call it honest money, Miss Prine. I got it doin' the hardest kinda work.'

Socrates didn't mind Luvia's hard stares. He knew that he was a bad man and so deserved her distrust.

'And ask'im to give Right somethin' for the pain. He'd be comfortable if they'd let up on some morphine.'

It was the sadness in his voice, he was sure, that enticed her hand out to take the money.

'I'll call'em,' she said. 'An' I'll go down with'im. But you know it wouldn't be no problem if he'd just go down to the veterans' hospital.'

'But he don't wanna go down there, Vi. You

259

wanna die in some strange place far away from where you live?'

'It wouldn't be strange if we were there with'im.'

'But it would be if it was night and we couldn't stay with him. Suppose he started dyin' in the middle'a the night? At least he'd like to know he could call you or me or somebody here.'

'It's God decides when you die and how, Mr Fortlow.'

'Then God must'a decided that Right's gonna die here with you.'

2

Blackbird Wills lived at Hogan's Snooker Room. He kept a bed in the back and took his meals at the bar. Hogan had disappeared years ago but Blackbird still paid the bills in the name of the corporation. It was said that Blackbird had killed Hogan and buried him in the basement. They had had a disagreement over a woman, Trisha Hinds, now Blackbird's common-law wife, and it had turned violent.

Nobody had loved Hogan and so the police weren't called. There were rumors, of course, but Blackbird paid his street insurance.

Hogan's Snooker wasn't an honest man's game. Guns moved through there; jewelry, illegal cellular phone numbers, and drugs too. The police got their

pockets lined. And so there was never a problem –
as long as nobody complained.

At night men would congregate there to meet
and plot. Blackbird knew all the robbers and
muggers and confidence men. Any professional
you wanted was there for the asking.

Socrates had never gone inside the doors. He
knew that a man was no better than the company
he kept.

But he walked into Hogan's place that Wednes-
day. He walked from the blazing sun into the cool
blue shadows of the Snooker Room. There were
a few men in the corner booth and Trisha was at
the bar. Hogan's Snooker Room wasn't the kind
of place that encouraged a healthy trade.

'Where Blackbird at?' he asked the woman, who
had obviously been beautiful at one time.

'Ain't you that man they call Socrates?' she
replied.

'Uh-huh.'

'They talk about you,' she said. Her eyes made
a survey of his bulk and size, then her lips twisted
as if to say, *It's possible.*

'What they say?' Socrates asked, cursing himself for even being drawn into conversation at
Hogan's.

'That you a mothahfuckah, that's what.' Her
sneer was sex; the kind of sex that Socrates had
murdered over – once.

'Well,' he said slowly. 'Today I'm just lookin'
for Blackbird.'

'What you want him for?'

'Go get him now,' Socrates said. 'Go on.'

A look of surprise set itself on Trisha's face; surprise that she was moving to do what Socrates asked. She wasn't the kind of woman to obey a man, not straight out. But she moved anyway, leaving Socrates standing at the bar.

He had a .45 in his pocket. It was a gun that he'd taken forcibly off of a boy in the park. It was for Right. The weight of that iron in his pocket made Socrates feel substantial and secure. Three days of a place like Hogan's and he'd be pulling liquor-store robberies; in three weeks he would use that gun.

'Yeah?' Blackbird said as he came up to Socrates at the front of the bar. 'What you want in the middle'a the day cain't wait?'

He was a tall man, well over six feet, and big-boned with heavy muscles and a long, deeply lined face. Blackbird had a lot of everything except neck. His head was right at the shoulder line and his shoulders were hunched up, making him look like a resting bird.

He looked down on Socrates and asked, 'Well?'

'I need sumpin' an' so I come here.'

'Who're you to come in here askin' for me?'

'I must be somebody,' Socrates said. ''Cause here you is.'

'Don't fuck wit' me, niggah.'

'You feel it when I fuck you, brother,' Socrates

said. 'I bust you open like a goddam watermelon.'

A series of emotions flashed over Blackbird's face and body. First he moved like he might throw a punch but then he stopped and distaste crossed his mouth. Socrates knew what was happening.

Blackbird was a bad man, and tough – probably even badder and tougher than Socrates himself. But Blackie was in a bind because his success made him vulnerable. He could fight Socrates, maybe kill him, but if he met with every man like that he'd end up in jail or with the Snooker Room burned down to Hogan's grave.

Socrates didn't have anything to lose. He could move on tomorrow and wouldn't be a cent poorer. All he owned was a few appliances from the Army surplus store and a plastic bag buried in his front yard. The bag was his bank, filled with almost fourteen thousand dollars that he got as a reward for turning in an arsonist.

All of Socrates' belongings could fit in the trunk of a Volkswagen Bug.

He smiled at Blackbird. 'Come on, man,' he said. 'Hear me out. That won't cost you a dime.'

'What?'

'I need a hundred tablets of morphine. The powerful stuff. For pain.'

'You come to me for that? Junkie, get out in the street. Get in the alley out back to score.'

'Don't do that, Mr Wills,' Socrates said in even tones.

'Or what?'

'You don't know me, man. You don't know who I am. But I am not to be played with. You got a business here and I got a right to come and do business.'

Blackbird laughed. 'Call the cops then. If you think I'm bein' unfair then you go'n call the goddam cops.'

'Oh,' Socrates said. 'I'm sure the police will come, brother. I'm sure they'll come all right. But we both know it's gonna be too late by then.'

Blackbird looked at Socrates. Maybe he remembered the stories of the man with killing hands who had come out of an Indiana prison. Or maybe he just saw the murder that Socrates could never erase from his eyes.

'Three hundred dollars for a hundred,' Blackbird said.

'I'll give ya four.'

'Four? Why?'

''Cause I ain't askin' no favors, that's why. You run a good business and I give ya a good tip.'

'Ha! You think a hundred dollars is money? Man, I could get ten thousand just like that.' Blackbird snapped his fingers loud as a gunshot.

'But right here,' Socrates said, 'right now, you gonna get four hundred dollars.'

3

'Oooooo,' Right Burke said at the corner of Hooper and Seventy-fourth. He brought his hand down to his lower abdomen and stopped.

'It hurt, Burke?' Socrates asked, as nonchalant as if he were talking about a bee sting.

'No, no,' the old man said. 'It's kinda like a, like a warm feeling. Damn. Them drugs do work, now don't they?'

The first three days Right slept like the dead – Blackbird's drugs allowing him to sleep soundly for the first time in weeks. He only woke up to take his pill and drink some broth.

On the fourth day he sat up and ate turkey and a chocolate bar.

On the fifth day he was walking on air next to his best and last friend – Socrates Fortlow.

'What you wanna do, Right?'

'I wanna go to a bar an' look at some long legs on a woman.'

Dilly's place was on Crenshaw, decked out in red Naugahyde and chrome. The girls who waited there wore hot pants that crawled up their butts and smiled at everybody just as if they were having the time of their lives.

Right took his evening pill with a mouthful of scotch. He smiled and said, 'Shit, this whiskey makin' me see double, Socco. An' you know that one'a you is plenty ugly enough.'

Socrates laughed. The .45 was still in his pocket. It had been completely rubbed down and wrapped in plastic. It would be his last gift to Right. But he was saving the surprise for later.

'You know why I like you, Socco?'

'No, man. No.'

''Cause you don't know no better.' Right laughed. 'They done whipped yo' black ass so bad that it don't never stop hurtin' an' there you are worryin' 'bout gettin' a job, 'bout these stray kids out here in the street. Here you come with my medicine when the clinic say they won't let them kinda drugs out in Watts. Can you believe that? Keepin' drugs out the ghetto by makin' sure sick people cain't get 'em. Damn. It's just about time t'die.'

Socrates sipped his drink.

'Ouvrez la porte!' Right shouted suddenly and loud. 'That's what we used to say in Paree. Ouvrez la porte! Open up goddammit 'cause Uncle Sam is here! An' they let us in wit' wine they done hid five years from the Germans. Opened up they wine cellars, they larder, an' they dresses too. Damn! That was sumthin', man. Seven thousand miles away from Arkansas, a gun in my hand, and a sweet woman on my lap. Mm! You know I coulda died right then . . . I shoulda died.'

'Naw, man,' Socrates said. 'We woulda missed you, brother.'

Right looked at his empty glass.

266

Socrates signaled for another drink.

'I'da missed you, Socrates Fortlow. Yes sir I would too. You always askin' them questions an' doin' all that kinda crazy stuff. You better than the movies; better'n the TV. You know I always felt bad when we'd be talkin' 'cause it seemed like you always thought'a everything already and was just testin' the rest'a us. That's how it seemed to me. I mean, I know you're my friend. I know you respect me too. But it was always you, always you.'

The waitress, a light brown and freckled girl, placed glasses before both men. Right took a deep drink and put down the squat glass.

They were seated in a posh booth but neither one was dressed for the occasion. Most of the patrons at Dilly's were young and decked out. Ladies in low-cut blouses and short skirts and their men in shiny grays or slender blacks. The music was modern-day crooning, sex set to song. Red lips wrapping around the words the way men wanted them wrapped. It was sexy and swinging and Right Burke held up his face to the din like a child letting the rain play on his skin.

He put up his good hand and a young woman in hot pants appeared.

'Uh-huh?' She smiled. There was a gap between her front teeth.

Right took two bills from his pocket; a fifty and a twenty. It was money that Socrates had loaned him. The girl looked into his eyes.

'Darlin', what's your name?' Right asked.

'Charla,' she said.

'Charla, this here fifty is for all the scotches we want. And the twenty is for you to bring'em here to us on time.' Right held up the bills and smiled.

He wasn't a handsome man, hadn't ever been. Stroke had partially paralyzed him. His left hand had been deformed into a useless tangle of twigs and half of his face was a permanent dead man's leer. Right limped, was missing three teeth up front, and weighed no more than a child. But still there was charm in his eye and flash in the way he cocked his head.

Charla, Socrates thought, was smiling more at his flirting than at her big tip.

'Yeah, Socco,' Right said when Charla went to get more drinks. 'I never had anything to say that you didn't already know. But I do now.'

'Yeah? What's that?' the big ex-con asked. He was happy to see his friend playing and talking. He was happy that Charla came over every few minutes to smile and show her long legs.

'Death,' Right said. 'I could tell you about death.'

In spite of himself Socrates leaned forward.

'Uh-huh.' Right Burke smiled with the knowledge that he had intrigued his hard-bitten friend. 'It's clear as day, brother. Cold and clear. It's like, it's like there's one world here and then there's another one. But they both in the same place. One of'em is hot an' sweaty but the other one is cool an' smooth.'

'You scared, Right?'

'Scared'a pain. I am scared'a pain all right but not no death, not no more.'

'You mean you put it outta your mind?' Socrates asked.

Right's eyes were like glassy brown-and-yellow marbles. He showed his few teeth in a smile.

'Naw, man. I know what you mean. You mean like when you in a war an' people be dyin' ev'rywhere. The shootin' an' the bombin', an' the flu too – cuttin' 'em down like flies. Your best friend dies an' then yo' new best friend dies. Happens ev'ry day. It's like automatic; your worry bone just shut off. You ain't scared no more. That's war. I bet it's life in jail too. But it ain't what I'm feelin'.'

'Maybe it's just the dope, Right. Maybe that's all it is.'

'Uh-uh, Socco. No no. It's not that. Even before you got me them drugs I could feel it. Late at night laid up in the bed with the ice pack on my belly. If I laid real still the cancer got quiet too. And I could feel it.'

'Feel what?'

'It was like somethin' was movin' in my body. Like I was dyin' and somethin' else was comin' t'life. Icy silver snakes movin' up an' down my body; singin' and slidin' along. If I got real quiet the feelin' would take over and anything from the real world, from the livin' world, would shock me

269

like I was in pain. It's like as if I had gone a long way and then I got dragged back and got bruised an' scuffed.'

'Is it your birthday?' Charla stood there with a glass of scotch in either hand.

Socrates glared at the girl. He wanted more from Right.

'Naw, honey,' Right said. 'It's a goin'-away party. I'm goin' home to my fam'ly.'

'Where's that?' she asked.

'Down south a ways.'

'Oh. That's nice. When you leavin'?'

'Later on tonight.'

4

They drank their scotches and then Right slammed down his glass. There was dancing music playing now. The young people were up on their feet and in each other's arms.

'But I, I couldn't let go until now, Socco.'

'No?'

'Uh-uh. When you die there's all this stuff gotta get done. Things you gotta say, things you gotta give away. It's hard work, man, and there you are busy listenin' t'them snakes.'

'Anything I can do for you, Right?'

'You already done everything you could do for me. I mean you got me morphine tablets, straight scotch, and pretty girls to watch. Shit, that's all a dyin' man could ask.' Right retched and turned to his left. He vomited a milky yellow fluid into the corner of the booth.

'Here,' Socrates said, throwing his napkin toward the corner. 'Cover it up.'

Right tried, and was mostly successful, but he didn't seem to care very much.

'You wanna go, Right?'

'In a minute, Socco. First I wanna tell you about what I done. And then I wanna ask you somethin'.'

'Okay. But you know Charla ain't gonna be smilin' too hard if she see that mess.'

'I got a in-surance policy, Socco,' Right said. He was sweating now, his good hand was shaking. 'Twenty thousand dollars. You get five and Luvia get the rest. She know about it. All the stuff in my bottom drawer is yours. Luvia know that too. And there's some letters to the boys, you know, Stony and Ralph and them.' As Right spoke his voice drifted off as if he were thinking about something else.

'Right,' Socrates said. 'We better go, man.'

'What you think about me?'

'Say what?'

'I wanna know what you see when you look at me, Socrates. I always wanted to know, but a man cain't ask that kinda question of another man. But now I can.'

'What you want?'

'I want you t'tell me what you see when you see me.'

'I don't know, man. You my friend. That's all. My friend.'

Right smiled and nodded, waiting for more.

Socrates didn't want to say any more though. He didn't want to be in that room full of young love and loud music. He didn't want to be drunk. He didn't want to watch Right die.

'I don't know, Right. What you want me to say? You my friend. My friend . . .'

Charla came up then and asked, 'Is he sick?'

'Yeah.'

5

Holding Right up, Socrates walked from the loud club. He went out to a bus stop on Crenshaw and sat.

'I'ma go get us a taxi, Right. You just wait here.'

But Right put out a weak hand and stayed his friend's departure.

'Let's just wait for a bus, man,' he said. 'I like the lights movin'.'

They sat for a few minutes in the noise of the street. It was about ten. There were lots of cars droning and honking and blaring loud music. There were sirens and swooping helicopters and blinking neon signs.

Socrates was afraid that the cool of the evening would kill Right.

'That's okay, Socco,' the old war veteran whispered. 'I know what you see.'

'Say what?'

'I know you love me, man. I love you too.'

'Yeah.'

'Help me get my pills,' Right said.

Socrates fished the bottle out of his friend's pocket.

'Pour me out ten and then take it away.'

Socrates did what he was told.

They sat after that for a long while. Right closed his eyes and slept or maybe, Socrates thought, he died.

When the bus was coming he shook Right's shoulder and the old man sat up, a little stronger.

'Come on, old man,' Socrates said.

Instead of accepting the help, Right started putting the pills one by one into his mouth. He'd swallow hard and then take another while Socrates watched.

'What you want me to do, Right?' Socrates asked when the bus was almost to them.

'Lea'me here, man. Get up on that bus an' go.'

'I cain't just leave you here, Right.'

'Why not? You cain't save me, Socco.' Right threw another pill into his mouth and swallowed. 'Just let me die, man. At least lemme have that.'

'But you my friend, man. You my friend. I cain't turn my back on no friend.'

'That doctor you sent me to told Luvia that I'm almost dead. He said that there wasn't no drug or no operation gonna save me.' Right was looking into Socrates' eyes.

The light over the dying man's shoulder turned green.

'An' this here, tonight, is the best I'm ever gonna feel again. Drunk an' high. I can still smell that waitress.' Right held up his gnarled hand. 'Let me die wit' sumpin'.'

The bus was almost on them.

Socrates wanted to do something but there was nothing to do. There was nothing to say. Right had said it all. He'd said it in his strong voice, the voice he used when he wanted to emphasize his manhood. It was that tone that made Socrates know he had to let go.

The bus stopped with a flatulent hiss and the doors levered open. Socrates stood up, felt the liquor in his head and staggered onto the steps. He turned around and grabbed the door to keep it from closing.

'Hey, man, what's wrong with you?' the driver shouted. 'Let that door go.'

Right smiled, actually showed his teeth, and waved at Socrates.

Socrates backed up into the cab, the doors slammed angrily, and the bus carried him away. He tried to get to a window, to wave one more goodbye, but the bus was crowded and by the time he'd reached the back he was too far away to see his friend.

The bus sped headlong into the dense night.

More than once Socrates reached for the buzzer, intent on getting off and running back to his friend. But every time he pulled his hand away. He thought of Right gritting his teeth and wilting to the side; he thought of the .45 in his pocket and the power to end his own life.

'He don't need no police car or hospital,' Socrates muttered. 'He don't need none'a that shit. And neither do I.'